Robin Llywelyn was born in 1958 and raised in Llanfrothen, Merioneth(now part of Gwynedd). He was educated at the University College of Wales, Aberystwyth. His first novel *Seren Wen ar Gefndir Gwyn* won the National Eisteddfod Prose Medal at Aberystwyth in 1992 and also the Welsh Arts Council's Book of the Year Prize and the Welsh Academy's John Griffith Williams Memorial Prize. His second novel, *O'r Harbwr Gwag i'r Cefnfor Gwyn* won the National Eisteddfod Prose Medal at Neath in 1994 and the BBC Writer of the Year Award the same year. This translation by the author of his second novel is the first time that his work has appeared in English. A grandson of architect Clough Williams-Ellis, he has worked at Portmeirion, Gwynedd since 1983 and lives close by with his wife Sian and their two children, Lowri and Iwan.

PARTHIAN BOOKS

*By the Same Author*
Seren Wen ar Gefndir Gwyn
O'r Harbwr Gwag i'r Cefnfor Gwyn
Y Dŵr Mawr Llwyd
*Published by Gwasg Gomer*

Places. Y Man a'r Lle 1 : Llanfrothen
*Published by Gwasg Gregynog*

# FROM EMPTY HARBOUR
# TO WHITE OCEAN

ROBIN LLYWELYN

PARTHIAN BOOKS

Originally published in Welsh as
*O'r Harbwr Gwag i'r Cefnfor Gwyn*
by Gwasg Gomer 1994

This translation first published 1996 in Wales by
Parthian Books
41, Skelmuir Road, Cardiff CF2 2PR

ISBN 0 952 1558 2 6

The publisher gratefully acknowledges the support of
the Arts Council of Wales in the translation of this
book.

Typeset in Galliard by JW.

A CIP catalogue record for this book is available from
the British Library.

Printed by Epic, Dorchester.

*For Euan and Susan*

*S*omewhere in the midst of the city's twilight a telephone rings in an empty room. The ringing falls like memories down the hallways and up and down the stairwells but does not permeate the heavy doors of the other apartments or their television laughter. In that bare room the phone's alarm bounces from wall to wall and echoes off the windows. Despite the ringing a stripe of white light that has fallen from the window remains still, dividing the floor into two and cutting the walls into grey triangles. In the shadows under the window the urgent machine calls from its perch on a mound of old directories. Next to it is an address book: one with a white-topped pencil in its spine and a frayed ribbon protruding from its torn pages. Other than that, and a few scrunches of screwed-up wrapping paper in the corners, the floor is empty. Out there, beyond the windows, the square trunks of the concrete forest rise up from the streets below where streams of red and white flow across six lanes. White smoke blows from the tops of buildings. The telephone rings on. Between two rings a siren whispers through the sound-proofed glass. For whom is this empty evening telephone calling out in vain? Whose heart is reaching out where no one waits to hear? Perhaps someone somewhere gets fed up with waiting - the ringing in the apartment suddenly cuts out. The siren's wail wells weakly and is swallowed by the night. At long last the apartment can readjust to tranquillity and start again to slip under the layers of dust that are already gently settling like flakes of snow upon the moor.

I am no expert at drawing pictures but this one is quite simple. All you need is a blue sea and a yellow sun. You need to see the docks, of course, and a rusty red ship moored along the quay. Spreading out from the quayside are acres of stacked containers, row upon row of them shimmering in the sun. Beyond lies the city reclining on a pillow of hills. On the quayside a nervous crowd spills in a ragged semi-circle from the shadow of the ship. The soldiers close in on them, like dogs working their flock into a sheepfold, forcing them back from the sunlight that falls on their heads, back to the shadow of the ship where the light fades from their teeth. Over on one side barking is heard and shots ring out. The smell of gunfire floats by. A commotion of voices and footsteps ensues as heels hit the wooden walkway back towards the gangway. More shots crash closer to the ear, bullets going skywards perhaps, but they still take fright. They stampede back across the gangplank. Into their iron sheepfold. The rest of the flock are not long after them, hauling their bundles back into the worn-out pasture of rusty tin. Only a very few, some of the ones who came without family, manage to evade the militia's shepherds and creep unnoticed to hiding places among the grid of stacked containers up behind the quay.

One of these was Gregor Marini, a trainee architect from the other side. He had been in two minds whether to chance it or not. His dreams of a new future made him feel sick. Who but an idiot could have thought, as he had, that all there was between him and a better life was day and night and a carpet of sea? He would go back, like a beaten dog. He would return to search again. For opportunities that did not exist. To hammer on doors no key would fit. Back to Alice to talk about the qualifications of his empty hands. The sun beat down. Through narrowed eyes he could see the crowd being sucked towards the ship. He winced as the hot metal of a container burnt his back. Two steps and he would be out of sight. He saw his opportunity and could not move. He was given no second chance. Vice-like hands grasped him. He was plucked into the gap between two containers and a rough hand closed on his mouth like sandpaper against his lips. He could see nothing, could not breath, could not cry out - to struggle seemed pointless. He yielded to the hand that grasped his face.

'Follow me, Gregor, and don't stumble,' said a grating voice in his ear. His eyes, grown accustomed to the shadows, made out a dark face beaded in sweat glaring at him inches from his nose. He saw two light-blue eyes under heavy brows staring at him. The hand was taken off his mouth.

'Petrog!' he said, gulping air.

Having crawled among the containers a good field's length from the quay they found an empty metal box twelve metres by three and climbed into it.

'What's your game, Gregor?' demanded Petrog. 'Trying to attract the soldiers' attention or what? You've got to take your chances when they come to you, mate. You'll go nowhere dawdling about like that.'

'I know,' admitted Gregor as he tried to get the container doors closed without rasping.

'Don't close it tight,' advised Petrog. 'Leave it ajar. Look, use the chain up there and be quick about it.'

Once the doors were pulled together it was dark as an eclipse but with the temperature rising. Gregor was beginning to regret that he had not followed the others back into the ship.

'How do we get out of here, Petrog?'

Petrog was sprawled on the floor with his face to the bright crack of the door. 'Wait till evening,' he replied nonchalantly. 'It will be easier now that there's two of us, easier to confuse them, I guess. Got any money?'

'A bit,' confessed Gregor fingering the paper currency in his pocket. He was thankful that most of it was sewn up tight in the lining of his jacket. 'That's all I've got.' He handed Petrog two ten-dollar bills.

'H'm, they're worth something over here,' said Petrog

getting to his feet. 'Hey, take a turn at the door to get some fresh air.'

Gregor rolled over to face the door and sucked in the feeble breeze which managed to slip through the gap. He tried to work up some saliva in the back of his mouth to moisten his tongue. Between his face and the steel he placed his neckerchief. He drew his hand across his face and his chin. The sweat was oily on his skin. He rubbed his nose between finger and thumb and filled both nostrils with the bitter-sweet aroma of his sweat. Did that help assuage his apprehensions? He pushed his fingers comb-like through his hair, shook his head and went back to staring through the gap in the door. Was he doing the right thing? What was he doing in a place like this in the first place, knowing nothing, knowing nobody? 'Petrog,' he croaked, 'what will become of us?'

'Shut up with your moaning,' said Petrog. 'As soon as we're over the fence there'll be no stopping us. It'll be full speed ahead to the Capital States once we're over.'

Gregor turned his face towards him but could not see him. 'What if we're turned back when we get there?'

'Listen, Gregor, with your attitude no one would ever have got anywhere. Anyway, it's only a tourist border between the North Country and the Capital States, not a real border. The worst bit is behind us.'

'Is it now?' said Gregor turning back to the shimmering light through the slit in the door. Perhaps a stray cloud had pacified the sun, as he could now see as far as the quayside without blinking. He could make out the source of the clanking chains, and he heard the hum of engines. The humming grew stronger until it became a growl and he detected the sound of water churning. The ship's horn blew long and hard as Gregor saw her gradually pull away, as slow as the minute hand on a tower clock. He followed the white path which spread behind the vessel and imagined the smell of the breeze over the cold foam. The red ship was a toy on a blue carpet, turning by degrees towards the harbour mouth. He strained to hear the seagulls' shrieks but the breeze must have changed.

Petrog was next to him with a stripe of sun across his face that lit up one eye. The stubble was dark on his chin. 'I need to breathe as well, you know.'

Gregor gave up his place at the door. Petrog put his lips to the opening, drinking greedily from the foreign afternoon.

As the sky turned a deeper shade of blue and the waves began to lose their shine, the cranes' long shadows made snail's paths across the concrete and the metal boxes. Gregor was slipping in and out of troubled dreams. Swallowing and swallowing from a bottle of sparkling water, the water streaming down his face but not quenching his thirst. He was sitting at a pavement table by the Aircol Hotel. Architects' plans formed the table cloth and on these stood an empty glass. Gregor was calling to the waiters for more water. Didn't he know them all? Were they not his colleagues? There was Steffan, yes, and over there was Zwingli. But none of them seemed inclined to notice him. He watched the occasional person crossing the beach below. Seagulls were diving in the wind. At last Steffan brought him his bottled water on a tray and set it before him. But each time before he could take a draught Zwingli's hands would come to snatch it from him. Another bottle would eventually be brought, but the same would happen. He was running from the hotel as fast as his legs could carry him. Was anyone chasing him? He was running from the town to the fields that rise above until the sea was far away below and the yellow eyes of the gorse followed him from the dikes. And here was the wood and the crystal stream gurgling between smooth stones and the sun flowing white in the foam. He threw himself down the banks and dipped his head into the shuddering depths until his head was filled with its deep rumbling noise. Gulping and swallowing with all his might and still there was no release from thirst. Drinking until his stomach was bursting and still needing more. All the water in all the world's rivers will not slake this burning drought. A great black heat fills his body, pressing it down like a lead weight as daylight recedes. His inside is a dark Ferris wheel turning without end and his eyes see nothing but bubbles coming from the depths. A claw closes on his arm and drags him in its pincer grip through the dark acres. It is dragging him to the cave on the ocean floor. He kicks and he struggles and awakens into a black world.

'Awake, are we?' Petrog released his arm with a dismissive shove. 'About time too.'

'Where are we?' Gregor could barely draw his tongue across his teeth. Then he remembered. Through the gap in the door he could see the moon's silver patchwork bobbing up and down in the bay. Sleep had not refreshed him.

'It's time to go.' Petrog put his arm on Gregor's shoulder. 'We'd better share out the money now, just in case. Ten dollars each will be enough for now in a place like this.'

A shudder went through Gregor as the door screeched open. Someone must have heard it. Or was it only in his head that the noise was loud? Was that the crunch of heavy boots outside? Or simply the rasping of waves on a pebbled shore? They both sprang from the box and crawled through the shadows.

Having reached the edge of the container terminal, they found themselves facing a wide open area far from the line of cranes along the quay. A flat expanse of tarmac stretched into the distance, warm acres bathed in moonlight. Once out in the open the low moon made their shadows dance like puppets in front of them. The sound of their footsteps seemed to fall around them like summer rain. On one side, the rectangular port buildings were dark except for the occasional square of yellow window. They heard a snatch of laughter on the breeze and the sound of glass breaking.

'We'd better split up,' hissed Petrog.

'What do you mean?'

'Split up. Twice as hard to catch two. I'll pay you back the money when we get through.'

'But Petrog...'

His companion was already moving away from him under

an orange circle of sky. They parted like two beetles separating on a village square. Gregor was on the verge of running after his friend when a searchlight clicked on and lit up the night. Gregor dived to the floor. Beams of light came from several directions, cutting through the night air like windmill blades. He saw the light come to rest on a moth of a man caught in a candle flame, his ragged clothes hanging from him like a sack. Voices barked, dogs growled, a loudspeaker shouted commands. He saw Petrog slowly raise his hands.

Gregor lay still as the soldiers milled around his companion. Their boots echoed all around. He ventured a peek towards the shadows beyond the open space. Inch by inch he hauled himself snake-like along the ground away from the animated throng pressing around his friend. His instincts drew him away, over towards the huts whose silhouettes gradually came into view where the open space met the fence. He did not look back; he concentrated on this slim path to freedom. His fingers found a purchase on the walls and his body slithered silently to the roof of a hut close to the wire. Between two hockeystick-shaped concrete posts he spread his jacket on the barbed wire which overhung a dark lane below. What did it matter that he tore the sleeve as he jumped?

He remained crouched down for a long while before he stood. Warehouses. Goods yards. Nobody about. Lights in the distance. Wide dark streets of stone-built houses with curtains drawn. Beyond, lighted streets offered crowds, anonymity and a place to eat.

The evening streets were busy. Car headlamps shone like sun on a water-wheel as the pedestrians wove their unseen pattern in and out and up and down the sidewalk. Globe-like street-lamps hung from intricate cast-iron brackets fixed to the buildings at even intervals all along the street. Underneath, neon advertising signs flashed red and blue. Gregor let himself be drawn into the crowd and yielded to its flow like seaweed on a swelling tide. He noticed a grand-looking lady with a lap-dog under one arm standing on the edge of the pavement with her free arm outstretched. A huge white cab pulled out of the stream of traffic towards her. Two lovers arm in arm walked wide-eyed and smiling, probably talking of things Gregor felt he would not understand. She was beautiful; his chin was smooth. He had curly hair; she flashed her teeth every time she smiled. On her head a white coif bobbed up and down as she walked. The lovers stepped back as a crowd of uniformed militia lurched by. One of them shoved the curly haired lover in his back. There was boisterous laughter. An innkeeper wearing a black apron stood hands on hips in a doorway. Gregor was sure he was watching him. The innkeeper whispered in the ear of a tall bony scar-faced man who stood by his side. The tall man smiled an ugly smile, making the scar twist on his cheek. Gregor walked on, past a tramp with his arm up to his armpit in a concrete rubbish bin, his vast coat tied with string and his hair matted and wild. Gregor glanced over his shoulder to check that the inn-keeper was not still watching. There was no sign of him or of the other man. His accent would betray him if he asked for something in a tavern. His ragged clothes would be no help either. They might ask for his papers... he had to be careful until he found his bearings...

'Hey, you!' shouted the tramp.

Gregor looked around him to see who the tramp was calling. He took a step forwards and pointed to his chest. 'Who, me?' he asked.

'What the hell are you doing on my patch?' demanded the tramp. 'Go on, get lost, you're not allowed here!' The tramp turned back to his work, rummaging in the bin.

Gregor waited and watched.

'I had better luck on the other side of town,' he said casually, taking a few copper coins from his pocket.

The tramp wheeled around and brought his huge face close to Gregor's. 'Where did you get those?'

'Here you are,' said Gregor handing him a coin. He felt in his pocket for some more coins. 'I got these as well.'

The tramp bit the coin. 'What do you want?' His eyes searched Gregor Marini's face.

14

'Got a drink?'

'Yes, thanks,' said the bum.

'You can keep the money if I can have a drink,' said Gregor.

'Haven't got that much worth of drink.' He pulled a big brown plastic bottle from his coat pocket and held it up to the light.

Half full. Gregor took it. The warm, flat beer revived him and gave him strength. As it emptied, his grip crushed the plastic under his fingers. He pushed the empty bottle into the bin and offered the tramp his hand.

'Gregor's the name.'

'Llygad Bwyd,' said the tramp brushing Gregor's hand aside. 'Was it only the drink you wanted?'

'I could eat something.'

'Got any more money?'

'A little.'

'Come on then.'

Having shoved their way through the crowd, they reached the quiet backstreets. Gregor wondered about the black dust that clung to the stone buildings making the place seem old. As they wandered down towards the dark end of the street he turned once to see the square of light with people moving across it where the main thoroughfare began.

Shortly they came to a huddle of men pushing and shoving one another on a wide stairway leading into an anonymous building with long rectangular windows on either side of the stairway. In spite of the dark stains on the windows outside and the condensation within, Gregor could make out that it was full of people. Llygad Bwyd strode into the crowd which immediately made way for him, closing around him as he passed. 'Not you!' someone shouted at Gregor as angry hands hauled him back.

'He's with me,' said Llygad Bwyd, stretching a hand to Gregor and pulling him after him.

Once his eyes got used to the harsh strip-lighting that illuminated the interior of what appeared to be a dining hall Gregor noticed a hatch in one wall through which white-sleeved, pink-gloved hands were passing out soup and bread. They both soon received a similar ration and Gregor offered some money.

'That's for me,' shouted Llygad Bwyd above the din. 'The money is mine for bringing you here. The food's free.'

They found room at a long table in a corner of the packed hall and began gulping down their food. Steam rose from the coats of the diners and from their soup. The whole place was permeated with the smell of boiled cabbage and urine.

Gregor felt thirsty again.

'Beer?' laughed Llygad Bwyd. 'This is a temperance hall. There's a water tap in the wall over there.'

It was only later, somewhere in the backstreets, that they came to a beer stall - nothing more than a trestle table with several shiny fat plastic bottles on it. The beer seller stood on one side and about two dozen men shifted about unsteadily on the other. Llygad Bwyd took some more of Gregor's coins and pushed past the men. After a bit of pointing and haggling he returned clutching two heavy plastic bottles and a clear glass one. 'Here,' he said pressing one into Gregor's arms. 'By the way, there wasn't any change.'

They drank the first flagon there and then, watched by the men. Llygad Bwyd left a few centimetres in the bottom, screwed on the cap and chucked it towards the crowd who immediately started fighting over it. They could hear the quarrelling for a long while as they walked, passing the second bottle from hand to hand.

As they swapped slugs of the white spirit Llygad Bwyd laughed for the first time. He wanted Gregor to sing sea-shanties. Gregor refused. What did he know of sea-shanties? All he wanted to do was rest. They got to a desolate patch of waste ground bounded by a cement-faced wall.

'Here we are,' said Llygad Bwyd.

'Where?'

'Home,' said Llygad Bwyd. 'Of course, if the accommodation is unsuitable... the park benches are usually free this time of night... and those soldiers are always so nice to refugees...'

'Here is fine,' said Gregor. 'You actually live here?' He felt the side of a box that was up against the wall.

'That's my box.' Llygad Bwyd struck angrily at his hand. 'I've got a wife and family, you know,' he added, passing Gregor the remains of the white spirit. 'And a blasted stepson. So I'm not quite homeless, see. It's just that at the moment I'm a common wanderer of the streets at night. Don't you see the moon waxing? Would that not be enough to draw you wandering? I can do without the drink, mind. But he's no help, that boy! He's not my son. He's turned the old woman his mother against me. Left me here to sleep under the stars. Pass the bottle, will you?'

Gregor found it hard to get drunk; he was too tired. He wasn't that enthralled by Llygad Bwyd's life history either. In fact he didn't listen. Perhaps he should have. He went for a piss and by the time he got back the tramp was in bed. Gregor laid his head on a wad of papers and tried to pull some loose broadsheets across his body. He fell into dreams almost before he was asleep. The ground's cold bite only hurt when he woke - maybe two or three times during the night. While he slept he was walking Cae'r Dibyn sleep-walks above the old town looking for a path down. The whitewashed houses of the port rise in steps from the granite quay. In the windows he sees grey faces like old photographs peering at him from an album. Roof tiles rise above laurel leaves. A white gravel drive scrunches under foot as the house turns the corner. Alice's face is in the window, half-obscured by her breath on the glass. He walks back down the drive, down the road past the photograph faces. A cloud splits open spilling sunlight on the rooftops.

He woke to the touch of hands, his eyes met the face of Llygad Bwyd bent over him going through his pockets, standing with his feet astride Gregor's chest. Gregor turned away from the sight of his filthy toes poking out the front of his boots. The old man saw he was awake and sprang back with a, 'Come on, get up.'

Gregor got up. He put his hand to his breast to feel the satisfaction of his hidden pocket. Then he looked up and saw the city angular and hard. Beyond, in the distance, there were hills on which clouds caught and were divided.

Leaving the waste ground they came to a path choked with fallen leaves and flanked with trees encased in tall narrow cages all along the river flowing under arched bridges. They walked down towards the town centre as the sun came up. Chestnut trees, last to bud, first to fall. He watched a leaf spin on the river's skin.

It must have been quite early. There were few people about, and they probably had better things to do than stare at two tramps. Llygad Bwyd explained that today they would be searching the rubbish bins on the river walk. Gregor could share his patch, the spoils would be shared two thirds to him, one third to Gregor, and Gregor would pay for the food. 'Good bargain you got there,' said Llygad Bwyd. 'You'd get nothing otherwise.'

Gregor nodded. He supposed it was one way of making a living.

Gregor found a heap of magazines and weeklies, still current stacked on a bin lid. In the bin itself he found a ball of lime-green wool which he took. Lower down he came to a bag of half-eaten chips and the remains of a beefburger still in its yellow dome of Styrofoam. Everything wound up in his bag. In another bin he excavated a pair of pink gym shoes with no laces. 'These might fit him,' he thought.

'What the damn use are these?' shrieked Llygad Bwyd, flinging the shoes to the ground. He leafed through the magazines, his eyes tarrying on the lingerie sections.

'Those mags are current,' announced Gregor. 'I'll sell them, just watch me.'

He took them to an intersection and tried to accost pedestrians. Didn't get much luck.

'At the lights, dummy!' shouted Llygad Bwyd from his seat by the river walk.

Gregor made it to the traffic lights on Park Avenue and started selling car to car. This worked better as the drivers seemed willing to give up a few coins to dissuade Gregor from getting his finger-marks all over their cars.

Llygad Bwyd was obviously impressed. 'Not too bad,' he said, taking his two thirds. 'You're getting the hang of it. That meat in bread was okay, too, but next time I want one with ketchup on it. These shoes are too big.'

'Tie them with the wool.'

'You can't have lime-green laces with pink shoes!'

'Why not? Try them... There, you see, they suit you!'

'Rather stylish, actually,' said Llygad Bwyd.

They split up again. Gregor went up towards the market area with all the stalls. On one of them an old woman wanted to sell him some wrinkled vegetables and a couple of fat yellow apples all covered in brown spots. He wondered who had written her business plan. A little farther on he came to a second-hand clothes stall.

'Leave them things alone!' shouted the stall-keeper.

Gregor pulled out a ten-dollar note.

The stall-holder carefully put down his cigarette and got up. He started passing Gregor all kinds of jackets and shirts. Gregor traded in his old clothes and walked away in a white shirt with a satin black jacket and dark trousers. He was looking for a hairdressing stall.

Shaved and washed, and with an old travelling razor in his pocket, he was ready to meet Llygad Bwyd.

At the river Llygad Bwyd eyed him up and down. 'What's all this?' he enquired. 'Who paid for all this?'

'I'm not quite homeless yet,' said Gregor. 'So I'll not be

sleeping rough again tonight.'

'Do look at his nibs,' said Llygad Bwyd. 'Fur coat and no knickers, that's what you are. Where the hell will you be going in that rig-out?'

'I thought perhaps you might recommend somewhere, Llygad Bwyd. Somewhere not too formal, not too steep...'

'Somewhere that won't ask for your identity card, is it? Because you'll be needing one of them soon. And in the mean time, go to Ostán Laban. It's open day and night, cheap and clean with plenty of room.' He tried to explain to Gregor how to find it. Gregor tried to remember.

'You said about the identity card?' said Gregor before they parted.

'It's cash up front only,' said Llygad Bwyd. 'Pro-forma okay?'

'You want me to trust you?'

'Llygad Bwyd's word is as good as his word. And mine is the only word you got. Now, do you take it or do you leave it?'

'Words cost nothing,' said Gregor.

'Beggars can't be choosers.'

'Here's half,' said Gregor 'The rest you get when I get the card.'

Llygad Bwyd snatched the dollar bills from his hand and turned without a word. The first drops of a shower were falling into the brown leaves. Gregor watched him go with his pink pumps and lime-green laces cleaving through the fallen leaves on the path like a snow plough.

2

The smell of new-mown hay fills the breeze as she picks her way along the path by the stream. They are mowing Fron Olau meadow; she sees them now through the trees and sees the meadow round and green around them. The trees that bend over the meadow are in dark shadow. Their highest leaves are in silhouette against a blue sky and a white cloud. It's only when she reaches the field's end that the swishing of the scythes through grass is heard. The stubble scratches her ankles and her arms are heavy from balancing the pitcher on her head.

The scythes grow silent. The men rest on their implements, watching her as she comes.

'Has your Nain nothing better for us than water, Iwerydd?' teased one of the men wiping his mouth on his sleeve.

'Nothing to chew on while we wait for our meal?' said another.

'We'll be eating the grass or starving, way things are around here.' The third man laughed. 'How long till dinner anyway?'

Deicws Bach says nothing as the others tease Iwerydd. He is the last to receive the pitcher. She carries it over to him and their fingers meet on the cold red clay of the vessel. He drinks deeply and pours what is left over his head, the water flattens his curls and soaks his shirt and his red neck-cloth until they drip. 'Thanks, Iwerydd.' He hands back the pitcher, smiling. His teeth are so white and his eyes so full of light. She knows he likes to look at her, but this time she does not look away. Today she lets him look her in the eye. She smiles and turns away.

*The men are refreshed. Deicws like the rest of them spits on his palms and grabs his scythe. 'Let's go to it, boys,' he calls. 'We've got the lower meadow to mow before lunch.' The whispering of the scythes starts up again, the swathes of grass fall like dominoes as the men move forward side by side.*

*It's nice to walk along summer pathways with an empty pitcher under your arm and your heart light as the sun and hearing nothing but the warm buzzing of insects. A peal of laughter rings out from the field. She turns. Deicws waves his hand. His curly hair is dry now; she imagines his blue eyes searching out her own. They'll be down in an hour or so. She hurries on her way down towards the house to save Nain's scolding.*

And good riddance to you too, thought Gregor as he watched the tramp lumbering up the riverside path away from him. He breathed in deeply of the damp afternoon air, feeling that yesterday's oppressive heat was already fading far away. What a relief to have got away from Llygad Bwyd, got away from his grumbling and reproaches. It was good to be on his own again to watch the stars come out. No one could scold him now, no one was going to grab him by the arm and drag him to one side. He'd get an identity card tomorrow, if he could trust Llygad Bwyd, and if he couldn't, he was none the worse really, was he? 'You can't win if you don't play,' he thought to himself as he wandered down towards the town centre. In order to be sure, he decided first of all to find the place where he was supposed to pick up the identity card the following day. There was no one sitting at the pavement tables. The chairs were all stacked on the tables with their legs in the air and the umbrellas all closed. It was strange how suddenly the weather had changed, he thought. He imagined families taking their leisure here on sunny summer days, sipping white wine and laughing under a blue sky. There was something sad about these outside tables now, with raindrops hanging like bells from the upturned backs of the chairs.

Wherever he walked strange smells wafted around him:

fried food, spices, sweet sticky smells, and unaccustomed noises seemed to swim around his head. Even the dogs' barking sounded different in this country. He was getting hungry. If he got something to eat maybe the city would seem less unreal to him. From a street stall he bought some oily cubes of meat wrapped in a flat pocket of bread. There were hot seeds in the bread and the red sauce was also fiery hot and once he had eaten his food he was dying for a drink. He pushed the food wrapper into a concrete bin and strode into the nearest bar. It was dark and the throbbing of the sound system was good as no one could interrogate him with such a wall of sound around him. He downed his cold beer and got out, suddenly feeling very tired. His feet were lumps of clay and every joint in his body ached. What time was it? It couldn't possibly be very late - but the night had already fallen and the neon lights above the cafes and bars were being turned off one by one.

By the time he found his hotel the place was in darkness and the front door locked. He struck a match to see whether there were any instructions for late arrivals. Nothing. On either side of the main entrance were large stone pillars made up of squares alternating with a central cylindrical column. This struck Gregor as out of place and unnecessary, probably turn of the century, when a lot of the worst things were built. He raised and released the knocker and jumped back, startled at the booming noise it caused inside. A short while later he heard muttering and the creaking of bed-springs, followed by a light coming on behind thin red curtains in the right-hand ground-floor room. The hall light came on in turn and then the front door opened as far as a security chain would allow it. A flashlamp clicked and shone a beam straight into his eyes.

'What do you want?' demanded a grumpy voice from behind the light.

'A room for the night,' said Gregor, squinting and shielding his eyes.

'No room. Too late. Good night.' Her voice was angry.

'If you don't mind,' said Gregor slowly and courteously, 'I

23

was given to believe that you are open day and night and hardly ever full. You would hardly leave me out here on the streets?'

The flashlamp walked over him from top to bottom. 'Well,' she said a little less grumpily. 'What do you mean by arriving here at this time of night? Where are your bags?'

'They will be sent on tomorrow. I regret my late arrival, however I am not responsible for the reliability of the train timetables, or for the scarcity of taxi cabs in this city. Come now, madam, show a bit of hospitality to a tired traveller. Don't leave me shivering on your doorstep. You are, after all, in the hospitality business, are you not?'

'You and your fine words...' She sounded pensive. 'Without bags in the middle of the night...' In a few moments she continued: 'Well, you'd better stand back while I open up.'

She stood in the doorway in her white nightdress and her flashlamp pointing to the floor. 'I know you now,' she said. 'I'm sorry if there was any misunderstanding earlier on...'

'Don't worry about it,' said Gregor with a yawn. He was having trouble keeping his eyes open. 'If I might now go on up to my room, I will see you about the formalities in the morning...'

He was allocated a room on the fifth floor. It contained an iron bedstead, a cupboard, one table and a chair plus a big white sink. Above the bed a small window with lace curtains opened onto a back yard. He found that it did open, and by placing one foot on the head-board he could stretch out far enough to see a white ribbon of river winding through the town. Above, long dark clouds, thin as smoke, lit up as they crossed the moon. The slate rooftops shone. On the other side a mass of cast iron pipe-work clung to the wall by his window, merging with some iron steps lower down. Everything seemed black and hard. He pulled his head in. 'Maybe things will work out,' he thought as he climbed into bed in his under-clothes. He winced as his forearm touched the metal frame, and shuddered as he drew the clammy sheets over him.

The next morning, having shaved and washed in cold water, he went downstairs. His door opened onto a landing off the main staircase and he saw now that corridors led off it in several directions. Peering down the stairwell, he could see heads and shoulders moving about on the ground floor. Above him, the top of the stairwell was lost in murky shadows. He noticed that the corridor carpet had long since lost its pattern, with the sacking underneath revealed in several places. Although Llygad Bwyd had been correct that the place was not full, it was certainly quite busy. The thin partitions of the rooms did little to muffle the coughing and quarrels that went on within. On the stairs late risers bounced down two steps at a time; night workers dragged themselves upwards, their fingers white around the banister; people stood in doorways. The stairway was narrow; those coming up had to squeeze past those going down. 'Good morning,' said Gregor to someone he met on the stairs. He got no answer. Two night workers came up. They climbed towards him as if they were riding a tandem bicycle up a steep hill. He got ready to greet them, sure that they would say something. They said nothing.

On the last flight of stairs he was almost knocked over by a red-headed lad who rushed past him. Gregor just managed to grab the handrail in time. The lad didn't turn a hair, he leapt the last four steps and bounded out through the front door.

The landlady was waiting for Gregor outside the door to her apartment 'The books are all ready inside,' she said. Gregor noticed a little window next to the door; used to keep watch on the hallway, he assumed.

As well as the hall window, she had a wide sash-window overlooking the street. It was now pushed open a few inches, making the red curtains on either side rise and fall gently in the draught. To one side was a bed and opposite, below the hall window, a low desk laid out with open ledgers. 'Here they are,' she said making a sweeping movement over them with the back of her hand. 'Won't you sit?'

Gregor sat at the desk and pored over the lined pages.

'What exactly am I supposed to do with them?'

'Why, that's for you to say, surely. New to the job are you?'

'I don't understand,' said Gregor.

'Well, wasn't it you who announced yourself last night as a quality inspector ? You would not have got in here otherwise, my lad.'

'I said no such thing,' protested Gregor. 'I don't know what you're on about. What do I know about inspecting anything?'

'You're from the Office, though, aren't you? Why else would you be here? I've got nothing to hide!'

'I'm not an inspector. I'm a student.'

'Oh, well...' She leant over the desk to close the books. 'I don't like those silly inspections. You never get to know what they complain about. It's too much for me. My husband used to do all the paperwork... never mind, would you like some tea?'

'A student, you said?' She asked as she poured. 'And your things are being sent on, did you say?'

'Well, no, as a matter of fact they won't.' Gregor felt a warm flush to his cheeks. 'In fact I'm afraid I did tell you a little white lie about my luggage. You see I was rather embarrassed at having arrived empty-handed. The truth is I lost my luggage - in fact it was stolen - that's what I suspect - on the train down here as I slept. All I've got left are the clothes on my back, but I can pay for the room of course. I searched that train from one end to the other but they must have got off before I woke up.'

'College term does not start for a month, Gregor.'

'A month? Why, no, of course. That's exactly why I'm here now, I was hoping to find work in the city to help tide me over the coming term... This hotel of yours seems busy, Mrs Laban.'

'I see,' she mused.

'Tell me, Mrs Laban,' continued Gregor, his teacup held in mid-air a few inches from his lips, 'why are your lodgers always in such a hurry, too busy to give a word of greeting ? I was nearly knocked over...'

'Everyone is like that here, Gregor. Who knows what they get up to or where they go. Don't expect a greeting from the people who stay here; they wouldn't risk speaking with a stranger. I mean, what with all this talk of refugees - that's really what scared me when you turned up so late - I thought you were an inspector, see. If the inspectors found a refugee hiding here, who but I would have to take the blame?'

'Well, thanks for the tea,' said Gregor fishing in his pocket for some money. 'How much do you need for the room?'

'Come now,' said Mrs Laban waving the dollar bills away, 'that's not for me to say. The Office's messengers will let you know when it's time to settle your account.'

'Do they keep your accounts too, then?' Gregor put the money back in his pocket.

'They keep everything in the end, my boy. You'll be looking for work, then, will you, Gregor? Anything special in mind?'

'Not much,' Gregor admitted. 'I guess it's as hard to get a job around here as anywhere else. I'm not without qualifications, see: I can make scale drawings, do estimates, draw up bills of quantity...and I know how to sell wine. Is there much demand for skills like these?'

'No,' she said. 'And do you know why? It's the fault of those blighters from overseas. They'll do double the work for half the money - how can anyone compete? It's an absolute scandal. Of course, it's also who you know, my Adam says. He'll be home for dinner in a minute - he will help you.'

Gregor noticed a folding bed stacked against the wall in the corner of the room. Steam was rising from a pot on a stove by the window and the pot cover was just starting to clack up and down. It must be lunchtime, thought Gregor as the woman hurried to turn it down. It was time for him to go.

'My son works in the library,' she continued proudly as she wiped her hands on a cloth. 'He is very well thought of there.'

'I'd be honoured to meet...' At that moment the door flew open and in stepped a tall bony man with a white scar across his cheek. The man wore an open-necked shirt with a gold ingot on a chain nestling among the protruding hairs of his chest.

'Adam,' said the woman, 'this is Gregor Marini. He's been looking forward to meeting you.'

'What does he want?' growled Adam without looking at Gregor. 'Is he staying here?' He turned two sullen eyes on Gregor. 'No residents allowed in this room, thank you. This room is private!'

'Now, now, Adam,' scolded the mother. 'Don't take any notice, Gregor. Adam always gets bad tempered when he's hungry, don't you, little one?'

Adam proceeded to pull on each finger of his right hand causing them to make cracking noises.

'There, there, Adam,' said his mother, 'Gregor is a student looking for work until term begins.'

'Is he indeed!' shouted Adam angrily. He cracked the knuckles of his other hand. 'Well you had better be in the café across the road at six o'clock. Now fuck off, I want my food.'

It was nice to stride into the daylight after the damp smell of boiling potatoes in her room. It was an afternoon of sky and sun; the side wind was fresh rather than cold. Gregor felt reasonably confident that he knew his way around by now. He was looking for the back street with the terrace of cafés. At the river he walked the banks under the shadows of the chestnut trees. Circles of sun fell through the branches and danced in front of him. He filled his head with the smell of autumn and listened to the crisp whispering of fallen leaves. Sometimes he would kick them up just to see them turn. The river's current was smooth except where it broke into foamy eddies on the pillars of stone-arched bridges. The river flowed south.He crossed it to what he thought was the east. Or maybe this was the east, he didn't really know. A bridge led into a park of emerald grass and hydrangeas. The air smelt of rain on leaves. He hardly noticed that his shoes were getting soaked in the grass. The metal box seemed a long time ago. A newspaper kiosk stood in the corner of the park. He walked up. 'Today's paper,' he said in a stranger's voice. He took it to a bench. But his eyes could do nothing but swim around the pages as he began wandering the streets of his memory and looking in at all the windows.

It was lunch-time that Saturday at the Aircol. The satisfied tinkle of knives on china and refined conversation filled the room. Waiters' feet padded across monogrammed carpets. He complimented the American's choice of a Calon Ségur 1982 but frowned when the fat man said he was to open it at the table. If he could have decanted it in the back this fine mess would never have happened. Oh! they wanted it opened in front of them like it was some part of the show. Treating good wine like it was a toy. Was it the Sommelier's fault the cork was gone to bits? How did he know it was going to fly out spraying a shower of wet red crumbs over the white blouse of the lady next to the fat man. She started screaming. What was a blouse to her? She probably had tens of them - he only had one job. And what chance of another in such an area? Who would want the Sommelier who spilt the wine? Who wanted an architect with no means of practising? Well, he did at least know his wines. He might be given another chance. Some agreed; they were mainly the new recruits. The old hands shook their heads in doubt. Gregor did not know what to think as he stood outside Zwingli's office behind the Front Desk. He listened to the clickety-clack of the typewriters and wondered if they were already typing out his letter of dismissal.

'Gregor,' said Zwingli, raising a pair of steady eyes from the note on his desk. Gregor was not used to seeing him behind a desk. He usually saw him sweeping past with a number of assistants in tow. Gregor stood in front of the desk under the light in his dark uniform. He related everything as it happened, how they treated wine like a toy, how he was not to blame, how he was not a circus clown, it was all their fault. Zwingli listened, making notes with a pencil on the edge of the document in front of him. He waited for Gregor to finish.

'Gregor,' he said, 'if it were up to me alone... if the whole matter was in my gift, - because you know I am fairly satisfied with your progress...and as I say, if only it were a matter for me alone. But it is not, Gregor. These were important clients, Gregor, and you screwed up. It is out of my hands. We need to show that action has been taken. We are all answerable to someone, Gregor, there can be no exceptions.'

'I'm willing to pay for the blouse, sir,' Gregor offered. 'You can deduct it weekly if you like.'

'That won't be necessary, Gregor.' Zwingli ruffled through some papers. 'H'm... yes, I thought so. You completed your seven years to be an architect. There we have it, there's plenty of scope, isn't that what they say? What are you wasting your time here for? I wish you luck, Gregor. You'll be paid to the end of your shift tonight. Oh, and we'll need your cupboard. I'm sorry about all this, Gregor, and as I say, if it were up to me...'

His co-workers were either on a shift or out on the town. Gregor was grateful. He felt empty as he threw his things in a bag and looked around one last time at the room he'd shared these six months. He picked up his bag and walked out.

When he got to the yard he had to force his way through a boisterous queue of lads all trying to be first in line. 'Hiya, Gregor!' said one. Gregor saw it was the boy they called Coesau Hirion. Gregor didn't know his name.

'Trying for a job, then, Coesau Hirion?'

'Why not?' Coesau Hirion laughed in Gregor's face. 'But I won't get it. What do I know about wine?'

'I've heard you know how to drink it,' Gregor said as he walked on.

There are green benches on the pavement that runs in a semi-circle sweep above the beach opposite the promenade hotels. He had sat on a green bench for a long time with his beak in his feathers, only occasionally watching the waves moving towards the beach, and the walkers on the sand taking their dogs for a walk. It had happened too suddenly. And even now as he sat on another bench in a strange city he was still pissed off at the injustice. He didn't have much faith in Adam Laban's ability to find him work. He needed to head off for the North Country. Maybe he'd make something of it up there. Out of the bowels of the city a muffled bell tolled slowly. He remembered Llygad Bwyd and the identity card. The newspaper he left, unread, on the top of the bin by his seat.

The sun had come out. From downtown, the purring of traffic rose towards him. At the roadside the black exhaust coughed over him as he waited to cross. He turned back towards the river and followed the footpath back to the sidewalk cafés. The sunshades were out over the pavement, shading the tables. At some of them garrulous groups gulped glasses of wine or espresso. At others people read papers alone. He checked to see whether Llygad Bwyd was around. All he saw was a big lady with a pile of hair on her head dragging a tiny white dog after her. The lead got caught as the animal ran under a chair. She was pulling and the lap-dog was pulling back. 'Fifi, come back,' she implored, shaking the chain and the empty collar. Fifi was gone. 'Make the most of it, Fifi,' thought Gregor.

Although it was not that busy, all the tables had been taken. There was a couple sharing a bottle of wine. Better leave them be. Some anoraked crank with funny eyes was looking at Gregor. Best avoid him. Someone else reading the Financial Pages. Perfect. He wouldn't take any notice. The table was at the edge of the pavement, beyond the sunshades. The newspaper reader did not look up. It was a very small table. The chair was hard and its back was at such an angle that if he leant back his feet would be on the other man's lap. If he leant forward his face would be right in the man's paper. So he sat up straight.

Presently, he noticed a shadow on the table and looked up. The landlord stood at his shoulder, menu in hand.

'Black coffee and a toasted sandwich,' said Gregor turning

the menu over in his hands.

The proprietor snatched the menu from him and walked off. The man reading the paper lowered one corner to stare at Gregor for a second. Gregor noticed that he was not reading the paper but using it to shield a writing pad on which he was jotting down notes in tiny spindly ants' legs' handwriting.

Eventually the man folded his paper, pocketed his notebook and tossed a few coins on his saucer. Gregor was now able to put his feet up on the vacant chair. He started to wonder about his food. No one would have been made to wait like this in the Aircol. In the Aircol you got your order within three minutes or your money back - that was the promise. And there was no one faster than he was. Even Zwingli had to admit that. Well, there was no going back. He needed to be positive, he just didn't know what positive meant. He remembered how he used to sit on the benches of Rhodfa'r Môr with the idea fermenting in his head that he had to take his chances overseas. He had some hard currency from the dollar tips and a bit more he'd saved up for the so called big day. He remembered it well: 'Now I've lost my job, another postponement, obviously.' Alice said it didn't matter, but to him it did. He would show them, though. When he got back from across the sea they would all see. He would show them he wasn't good for nothing after all. He remembered how these thoughts would flit about his head as he sat on the bench outside the Aircol, waiting for his shift to end. He did not want to go early or Alice would know something had happened. Anyway, she'd always said he should try to get work as an architect. Some architect, he thought, he hadn't even been able to open a bottle of wine. That story would run and run. The work was gone and he was getting out.

When three o'clock came he dragged his feet up the hill, past the whitewashed houses ranked in steps up from the beach. Gulls screeched above his head. When he got there she asked what would he do now. 'I have no choice,' he replied. She wasn't keen. 'Even if our borders are open, the Capital States don't want people like us, Gregor. You'll get turned back.' 'Petrog said there's a boat.' 'Don't go, Gregor,' she said. 'We can work things out for you.' 'I don't need that.' 'When will you be back?' 'I'll write as soon as I arrive.'

He left her standing on the wide porch. His heels churned the white pebbles. Down on the street a sea breeze blew into his face.

'Your coffee,' said the landlord slamming a tiny white cup and saucer on the tin table-top. Gregor jumped and hit his knee under the table, making the coffee spill. 'Your toasted sandwich.' He struck a small plate down in the spilt coffee and tucked a bill under it.

'Excuse me,' said Gregor, picking up the bill. 'I was supposed to meet someone here today and...'

'Yes,' snapped the landlord. 'And it's usual to pay up front around here, not half and half, do you understand?'

Gregor felt something hard in the folded paper. Unfolded, a credit-card size piece of blue plastic was revealed. He checked the bill. 'Hey, that's more than I agreed,' he protested.

'The food and the coffee are extra,' said the landlord, his silver tray held firmly to his chest. 'Come on, stranger, pay up. I've got other customers to see to.'

Gregor paid. He drained the dregs of the coffee and grabbed the toasted sandwich. Once he had got a bit of distance between him and the café he examined the card. Not very professional, he thought. Someone had actually signed his name on the band. Nothing like his signature. He looked for a clock somewhere in the streetscape. A quarter to six already? In fright he legged it back to the river bank and followed its avenues down. Heavy gutted clouds hung in the sky and the lights were coming on in the harbour below. Did he know this area? He saw someone throwing crumbs to the pigeons and he ran up to him.

'Can you tell me where Ostán Laban is please?' he asked with his breath in his fist. The man made a slight sideways movement of his head and threw a few more crumbs towards the birds.

Gregor glanced where the man had gestured and saw Ostán Laban in electric blue lettering blinking on and off through the branches on the avenue. A big "OPEN" hung lopsided on the glass door of the café opposite.

The mechanical bell clucked as Gregor walked in. The café was hung with smoke. On the wall the clock was striking six. Adam Laban was at a table near the back drumming his fingers. When he saw Gregor he stood up and came forward.

'I'm sorry if I kept you waiting,' said Gregor as they met.

'Didn't I say six o'clock?' demanded Adam Laban. He marched out of the café and down the road, with Gregor running after him.

'Is the library far, Adam?' called Gregor.

Adam did not answer. Gregor could not keep up with him He lost him once, even thought of going back, but then caught a glimpse of him between two buildings. With a huge effort that made his heart ache he almost caught up; Adam just walked on swiftly as before. 'Yes, it's very far,' he tossed over his shoulder as he sped ahead.

'Can I come there with you, in case there's work?'

'That's what you're doing now, isn't it? And when I say six, it means quarter to, got it ?'

'Yes, chief.' Gregor felt he was beginning to be accepted. He followed Adam Laban down some subway steps through wide gates into a bare hall with benches all along the walls and one opening in the far side with the words 'THE LIBRARY' above it in black angular lettering. Gregor felt that underground was probably not a good place for a library, unless of course they had no damp problems in this country.

'Sit there,' said Adam. 'I'm off.'


It was more like an underground car-park. Bare concrete walls and ceilings, exposed pipe-work, naked lights. 'I expect the library is quite grand inside,' Gregor mused. The place was filling up. People were coming in, men and women of all ages, streaming in through the gates until their bodies began to warm up the clammy air. Soon condensation was forming droplets on the ceiling pipes and falling down to the floor. When the benches were tight with bottoms and Gregor was trying to lock his legs against the floor to avoid being squeezed like a pip, the outside gates were closed.

An official strode up to a lectern.

'Today's opportunities,' he announced, reading off from a clip-board. 'Weeders. Six with experience and not afraid of work. Word Department.' A lot of arms went up. Six were chosen and taken away.

'Burners. Two with appropriate qualifications. History Department.' Only three applied for this position and there was some dispute before one of them was turned away. He pretended to go out but actually slid back to the bench.

'Lying dogs. Twelve. Department of Politics.' Gregor noticed that the one who had been rejected before was accepted this time, as well as eleven lucky others chosen at random from an enthusiastic row of waving arms.

'Ash tray cleaners!' announced the official. 'Two to be under Adam Laban. Ash Tray Cleaning Department.' Gregor put up his hand.

He was too late. Two others were already being congratulated by less successful colleagues.

'Cataloguer. One. No experience required. Department of Mythology.' Not one hand was raised. The people seemed to plant their feet more firmly on the floor and push their backs against the walls, hands deep in their pockets, all staring at the floor. The official held a palm to his brow and scanned the benches. Gregor's hands were on his knees, his head was not bent. The official's eyes alighted upon him. Gregor slowly raised his hand.

Staff members came to fetch him and he was taken away. He heard the next announcement: 'Dog Walker. One. A thick-skinned skilled communicator required. Department of Taking the Chief Librarian's Dog for a Walk.' Gregor heard a commotion of feet on concrete and imagined that this was a good job.

It didn't seem to matter what job one tried for, the registration procedure was all the same. Name, age, address, qualifications. Gregor offered his new identity card but they did no more than glance at it, nod, and usher him through. 'This way,' said an official, prodding him.

'Stand there,' spat another one like a camel when they got to a high arched double doorway with one door open. Gregor could see nothing beyond the door but a kind of wooden pulpit. Presently a scratching noise came from the pulpit and a head covered with a mop of black hair rose up and a furious pair of spectacles framed two burning eyes that glared at Gregor. 'Come here!'

'Good-day,' said the hairy one in the pulpit accusingly. 'What have they sent me this time?'

'Gregor, sir. I've come to catalogue your department.'

'I am the Du Traheus,' said the furious pair of spectacles. 'I am head of this Department. I decide who does what. Do you have any relevant qualifications?'

'No, sir.'

'Can you at least read and write?'

'I am a student.'

'You avoid the question? Well, no worse than the rest I suppose.' The Du Traheus descended from his pulpit. 'Come,' he said shuffling across the floor like a chimpanzee, one large hairy paw wrapped around Gregor's wrist.

Gregor was put to work at a low desk piled with books. The Du Traheus drew a black fingernail over them. 'Register, classify,' he said. 'Both these words are better than the word catalogue'.

'Sorry?' said Gregor.

'It's not your fault, my boy,' said the Head of the Department, scurrying back to his pulpit and muttering.

# 3

The bagpipes' drone rises and falls as the ribbons on the hats whirl and the petticoats flow. Lines of dancers hand in hand weave in and out following the pattern of the dance. Black clogs strike the cobbles; dust floats in the air above the square; the smoke from meat-stalls smells of burnt fat. The last lingering note of the pipes fall away. The pipers reach down to their drinks; two musicians on two upturned casks on a village square. They glance at each another before beginning a fast moving dance. Deicws moves to the edge of the dance area. Other lads are also looking around for partners. He rubs a knuckle into the dust that clings to the sweat on his forehead.

Iwerydd waits for him to catch her gaze. Deicws moves towards her. 'Won't you dance, Iwerydd?' He smiles. 'It's not too hot for you, is it?'

'You're the one that's sweating, Deicws.'

Everyone always has a good time on the local Saint's name day. Most people seem to leave their worries behind. Others simply watch and follow with their eyes the various paths that come together on days like this; experienced eyes are poised to pick out new lives beginning. The tourists watch also, their video cameras at the ready.

'Another dance?' He keeps hold of her hand. She nods.

His strong fingers are gentle on her hand. His skin is strong and his step is sure. She moves with him step for step, leading sometimes, sometimes being led. A hundred pairs of wooden shoes hit the ground in unison. Smoke billows up from the cooking stalls. Wood smoke drifts on the air. T-shirted tourists in shorts follow it *with their cameras. She does not care. She's free now as she flows slowly back and forth and up and down, hand in hand with Deicws Bach. She smiles her white smile at Deicws as someone pokes a video camera towards them.*

*'Why do they want to take our picture, Deicws?'*

*'Because they don't see like we see,' he replies. 'Forget about them, Iwerydd.' They dance a few more steps. 'They'll get no pictures, anyway. We don't exist for these people; they don't see us at all. When they come to play their tapes there'll be nothing on them but an empty square and two upturned casks.'*

*'You and your teasing,' she said, holding on to his hand as the music ebbed away at the end of the dance. 'I've got to go.'*

*'When will I see you, Iwerydd?'*

*'I'll be at Rhyd-y-Felin at dusk.' She adjusts the coif on her head and smiles at him. 'Come to keep me company if you like.'*

*On the edge of the square she looks back at him. 'Rhyd-y-Felin,' he mouths.*

*As she climbs the cart road up from the village the mewing of the bagpipes gradually fades away below her. She cuts across the fields, through the trees up the side of the valley.*

One by one Gregor drew the books towards him and turned them over in his hands. He was starting to forget his empty stomach. 'What the hell am I supposed to do with these?' He looked up at the myriad shelves of books he saw in all directions...no beginning and no end, just shadows. He looked at the books on his desk, browsed through them, looked for a pattern. He drew five columns down a sheet of paper and a line across the top for his headings. Title, author, publisher, place and date. Surely that would do it. In a while he had filled the first page. He believed he could now venture back to the pulpit, where he saw a sliver of light, to look for his master and show him the work he had done.

In his pulpit the Du Traheus raised his head from his book and peered over his spectacles.

'So, you can write?' he enquired dubiously, taking the paper from Gregor's hands.

'Of course I can,' retorted Gregor indignantly.

'Well, that's excellent,' said the Du Traheus. 'We'd better celebrate.' He went to a cupboard in his pulpit and took out three bottles containing different coloured liquids. There seemed to be fruits of some sort swimming around in them. 'I take it you are not a practising teetotaller?'

'No,' said Gregor.

'Cherry brandy it is, then,' announced the Du Traheus. He poured a good measure into two glasses. 'Long live the old ways!' he said and clinked his glass on the glass of his disciple's.

'Health to the Bookworm!' added Gregor, hoping it was an appropriate response. The brandy was fiery and at first it burnt Gregor's throat.

They drank another dram each. Once the burning in his throat had passed Gregor began to feel quite cheerful. Perhaps the Du Traheus was not such a bad sort after all. Gregor plucked up his courage and asked, 'Is the work correct at all, sir?'

'No,' said the Du Traheus. He went back to his cupboard and took out a loaf of bread, a round cheese and a knife. 'Are you hungry?'

Gregor ate the bread and cheese he was offered. They finished the cherry brandy. The Du Traheus got out his pipe and filled it methodically. Soon a fragrant smoke was fanning out around him. He sucked on the stem of his pipe, occasionally striking it against his teeth. 'It's midnight,' he said. 'Your apprenticeship is over.' He climbed up into his pulpit and rummaged around. He then held up what Gregor thought was a small brooch or maybe a ring. It turned out to be a badge which he pinned to Gregor's lapel. 'There you are,' he said. 'Your badge of office.' It was shaped in the form of a ship under full sail with the legend Gregor Marini: Under-Cataloguer, Department of Mythology.

'Go now,' said the Du Traheus. 'It suits you fine.'

'Back at a quarter to, is it, sir?' Gregor saluted and stumbled towards the door.

An official touched his cap as Gregor left the bunker. It was raining outside. The tyres of cars wrung water out of the gutters and sent it slewing over the pavements. Webs of rain passed by the street lights, the drops freezing for a second before falling. Leaves squelched like wet paper under foot. He was passing the park back towards the café when he heard the nightingale. How he knew it was a nightingale he could not tell. He hadn't ever heard one before. Her song flowed over him as the prickly rain touching his forehead. He tried to catch a glimpse but could not find her. Something like homesickness gnawed his gut. She stopped suddenly and a flurry of wings told Gregor she was gone. 'Good luck to you,' said Gregor, imagining her beak cleaving a path through the falling rain.

Although it was late the café was open, a fug of smoke and fatty smells hit him as he walked through the door. Some people were eating breakfast, others were having tea. He got to sit between two night workers having lunch. He ordered a bowl of lobscows with bread and butter and a bottle of country wine.

'Howdy?' said the night worker to the left of him.

Gregor had to spit out half a mouthful of lobscows into his bowl. 'Well, fine thanks,' he replied, dabbing his lips with a napkin. 'And yourselves? It's a rainy night. I heard a nightingale singing earlier, did you know they...'

'All I said was "Howdy",' said the night-worker, stuffing a forkful of meat into his mouth. 'I don't want to hear your life story.'

'Sorry,' said Gregor, lifting his spoon.

How come if these guys did so little talking it was so loud in here he wondered. It seemed like most of the noise was coming from the back room. There was the sound of furniture crashing to the floor. Glass shattering. The commotion was increasing by the minute. No one in the café seemed to notice.

Gregor kept looking up, and eventually from the smoke in the side-room entrance he observed Adam Laban staggering with blood spouting from a hole in his head. Gregor rushed up to him, tearing a hanky from his pocket. 'Are you all right, Adam?' he cried as he dabbed the wound with his hanky.

'I was till I saw you,' said Adam Laban.

'I just popped in for a bite on my way home.'

'Home?' demanded Adam.

'Back to the hotel.'

'Back from where?'

'My new job.'

Adam Laban sneered. 'So they employed you, did they?'

'Under the Du Traheus.'

'Humph!!' said Adam Laban. 'What do you know about it?'

'Well, I did try for a job cleaning ashtrays but I was unlucky.'

'Unlucky?' said Adam Laban through his teeth. 'Luck had nothing to do with it. I didn't want you, that's why you didn't get it. I do not take work-shy riff-raff in my department. Apparently the Du Traheus does not set such high standards.'

'What happened to your head?' asked Gregor.

'Is this hanky clean?'

Gregor nodded. Adam dabbed the side of his head.

'Good-night then,' said Gregor. 'I'm off to get some shut eye.'

' "Shut eye"?' cried Adam. 'Why can't you just say "bed" like everybody else?' He turned on his heel.

Gregor watched him walk back into the smoke-filled room.

As he had no alarm-clock Gregor decided to stay awake all night. Unfortunately, he fell asleep about three o'clock in the morning and the first light of dawn was already at his window when he woke up.

He went straight to the café over the road. It was only just past five a.m. Even so, he gulped down his porridge and his cup of tea and legged it for the library. Once there, he had to shuffle around trying to keep warm, waiting for the gates to open at a quarter to. The wind seemed to breathe through him and his bones were cold. At last he showed his badge and in he went.

'What kept you?' shouted the Du Traheus from his pulpit when Gregor knocked. 'Come in, for goodness sake.'

'Does this devil live here all the time?' wondered Gregor. 'Good morning, Du Traheus!' he said.

'Is it?' said the Du Traheus, taking his spectacles in one hand and rubbing a knuckle to a tired eye. 'I'm dubious. Now, get back to work.' He perched his spectacles back on the bridge of his nose.

Gregor was sorry that he was doing it all wrong. However, as no alternative method had been suggested to him he carried on regardless. During his lunch-time he went over to the library's main entrance to look up the central register. He found Reference Department on the board. It happened to be quite close to his own department. He would only be a few minutes. He showed his badge at the door.

'I'm looking for the letter C,' he said to the door-keeper.

'Why don't you look between B and D then?' yawned the man.

'No, you misunderstand,' Gregor said carefully. 'I wish to find the section in which every word begins with a C.'

'Well look between B and D, then,' repeated the door-keeper making as if to get up from his deck-chair. 'What's the matter with you?'

Gregor went past cast-iron, castle, cast-off, castor-oil, skirted catacomb, catalepsy and finally stopped at catalogue. He got back to the Mythology Department with a couple of books under his arm and without the Du Traheus even noticing that he was late.

At his desk he found Adam Laban, idly chewing gum, with

his arms folded across his chest.

'Hello, Adam.'

'Where've you been?' Adam Laban got up and grabbed Gregor by the lapels. 'Turn that cheek so that I can give you one!' He straightened a palm to strike.

'Let me go!' Gregor shouted in alarm.

Adam shook him and flung him down on his desk. 'Sit!' he said, pointing.

Gregor squeezed himself back behind his desk. He had to squat down like a big spider in a little box. Adam sat on the corner of the desk, head lowered towards Gregor, as if waiting for an explanation. Gregor noticed that a black blob of blood had coagulated at the side of Adam's ear. He had obviously not washed or combed his hair. And he smelt of whisky and tobacco.

'What?' asked Gregor.

Adam pointed to his wrist even though there was no watch there. 'You are late!' he snarled.

'Better late than never, I suppose,' said Gregor. 'Anyway, the Du Traheus didn't say anything. And it's up to him, I think, isn't it, Adam?'

'Yes, and it's up to me to make sure that baboon runs this department properly,' spat Adam. 'You've held this department up for ten minutes with your wild gallivanting and you've caused the Du Traheus big trouble.'

'I don't believe it,' said Gregor. 'You're an ashtray cleaner. You're not his boss.'

'Come here.' Adam took hold of Gregor's wrist and dragged him like a rag doll back to the pulpit by the entrance. 'Come down here you, hairy ape,' he shouted up at the Du Traheus, who eventually clambered down and stooped before them, his knuckles sweeping the floor. Adam Laban picked up a heavy tome from a nearby table. The Du Traheus looked impassively from Adam to Gregor and back again. Adam weighed the volume in his hand. 'Books are terrible things for making you sleepy, don't you think?' he said, raising the book up high and then crashing it down upon the old man's skull. The Du Traheus fell pole-axed to the floor. He lay there with arms and legs spreadeagled, his spectacles spinning on the floor.

'Don't let this happen again, Du Traheus,' shouted Adam Laban, aiming a vicious kick at his ribs.

When he was gone Gregor fell to his knees by his master's side. He turned him carefully over on his back. Under his head he packed some paperbacks like a pillow. He placed the spectacles back on his master's nose. He got some brandy and poured two glassfuls, one of which he drank and the other he tried to pour down the Du Traheus' throat. Most of it went over his beard and clothes but some must have gone in as he began to stir and in a moment was calling for another glassful. 'That's better,' said the Du Traheus. 'Now,' he added, propping himself up on one elbow and wagging a scolding finger at Gregor, 'this must never happen again.'

'I promise it won't, sir,' said Gregor.

'Do we know what it is?' asked the Du Traheus'

'What, sir?'

'The thing that mustn't happen again.'

'Well, me coming back late from lunch, sir.'

'Oh,' said the Du Traheus picking himself up from the floor. 'Well that's easy. Don't come back late from lunch again, Gregor.' The Du Traheus dusted down his suit. 'I'm glad that's settled.'

'I'm very sorry I caused you all this trouble, Du Traheus. Is it really true he's your boss?'

'Who, Adam Laban? Well, that's what he tells me,' answered the Du Traheus dreamily. 'But everyone has to serve somebody in the end, even Adam Laban.'

'Does he clean ashtrays?'

'Only mine. I'm the only one in the library allowed to smoke. All the other departments are non-smoking, but I've retained my right to smoke my pipe whenever I like. I'm also allowed to keep bread and brandy in my cupboard. How else could I live here? It would be intolerable.'

'So you do live here?'

'I hear that Winter is on its way outside, but that doesn't worry me down here, does it? And I pay no rent. So what are a few blows from Adam Laban compared with all that?'

'Is he allowed to be insolent towards you?'

'No, that's not allowed.' The Du Traheus fingered the egg-shaped bump on his head. 'He's allowed to be impertinent, audacious even, but not insolent, according to my service contract.'

'But calling you a 'baboon' and a 'hairy ape' is surely insolent rather than impertinent, is it not?'

'Not at all.' He thought for a while. 'No, in this instance he was just being downright rude.'

'Well, you know the rules, I guess,' muttered Gregor and he slunk back to his desk, vaguely speculating on whether the Du Traheus was crazed, cracked, potted or just simply mad.

He learned a great deal from his borrowed books. Apparently he should have been using index cards, not sheets. He found the cards in the department's storeroom. He soon realised it was better to begin at the beginning of a shelf and work along it, rather than snatch up volumes haphazardly. Although the Du Traheus did not show much interest in Gregor's work, Gregor did his best to impress. He would work through his lunchtimes, stopping only for a few minutes to share a bite with his master and knock back some dubious-looking and highly alcoholic syrups referred to by the Du Traheus as 'brandy'. The only one who would darken his cramped desk was Adam Laban on his rounds when he came to empty the Du Traheus's ashtray.

Despite the deplorable lack of encouragement given by his head of department, Gregor managed during the first few days of his new card-index system, to catalogue quite a distance along several shelves. His desk was at the hub of book-lined avenues radiating out 360 degrees around the spot where he sat, like the spokes of a wheel. The only avenue that reached anywhere, as far as he could tell, was the one that led back to the pulpit and the exit door. He was delighted some days later when it was announced that he could have the afternoon off. Surely this was a sign that his diligence had been noted. He was allowed off on the understanding that he was needed for the evening shift at a quarter to. Six hours, he thought: almost a whole day. He needed some things. Underwear, soap, envelopes and paper, and a stamp. At one of the second-hand stalls by the park he asked the price of a big black old-fashioned radio set. It was not cheap, but it seemed to work, so he got it anyway. On another stall he haggled for a silver-plated ornate photo-frame. For his accumulating possessions he bought a second-hand leather hold-all and packed them into it.

As he set the frame on the table in his room he realized he had no photograph of Alice but at least the place was a bit more homely now. He felt like a magpie with his bits and pieces arranged around him in his cold nest. He extended the radio aerial and played with the tuning knob. Through the sounds of frying and squeaking, he heard words from his own country murmuring faintly. The whispers that reached him through the hissing of the airwaves made him feel far away from his life before. He turned the radio off and pushed it to the bottom of his bag. A piece of paper and a pen lay before him on the table. He realized that he had never had to write to her before. The words did not seem to fall easily on the page. She would be disappointed to hear the whole truth of the matter, and anyway, things might improve - why upset her for no reason? On the other hand, he did not want to raise her hopes either... in case it all came to nothing in the end. What could he say? He would let her know he had arrived safely, that he still loved her, that he was thinking about her and that he had a job already but was hoping to head North soon... Having addressed the envelope and stuck the stamp in place, he looked up to find evening shadows growing on the walls. Why the hell did they need a night shift anyway? It was only a library. On his way out he dropped the letter into the mail box next to Mrs Laban's apartment and then hurried on his way to the library for a quarter to six.

Gregor had decided he would tackle a whole shelf this evening, right to the end.

It would probably take a long time, even weeks - but eventually the Du Traheus would recognise his efforts. He would find that his assistant was on top of things, was an asset to the department, and he would finally get the approval he considered he deserved. First, to reconnoitre the task, he decided to walk down the length of one of the avenues.

Soon the light from the bulb above his desk was no more than a far off twinkle. The shelves were deep in shadowy, dusty darkness. Close to his desk the parquet flooring was covered with a thin layer of dust, but here the dust was thick underfoot, muffling the sound of his footsteps. Narrow book-lined ravines opened off the main avenue, their upper reaches lost to the eye. The twinkle of the light above his desk was gone. He did not remember turning a corner. He slid a heavy tome down from a shelf and positioned it as a milestone to guide him back. He walked onwards as dust swirled, clinging to his hair and clothes and to his sweat-soaked brow. Dust crunched between his teeth and irritated his tongue. There was no sound to be heard other than the slight crunching of his feet as if he were walking on powdered snow. He thought of the men who walked on the moon for the first time, leaving their footprints there for evermore; he thought of the crustacean collectors who walked the primeval estuaries, leaving their fossilized footsteps in the sandstone of an ancient shoreline. Not much chance of his footsteps lasting that long, he thought, as he sank up to his ankles in the dust. It filled his socks. It was in his pockets. Hanging cobwebs caught in his hair. He ran a finger along the front of a shelf and watched the warm trickle of dust flow silently like an egg-timer to the floor. Cobwebs blocked his way. He tried to brush them aside but the farther he went the tighter they wrapped around him. Grabbing hold of a heavy book he threw it towards the thickest part of the web. The book swung to and fro as if in a hammock. He threw another after it. The web broke and both books fell with a thud into the dust. It seemed like a good time to turn back. However, where he had previously struggled through the web, the strands appeared to have closed behind, obliging him to fight harder than before just to go back the way he had come. With no purchase for his feet in the dust he slipped and fell, and the weight of the net of dusty cobwebs forced him to crawl and then slither on his stomach like an eel in wet grass. He was relieved when he got back to the marker-book on the floor. His relief promptly disappeared when he came to another similar book on a similar cross-point and another after that. 'Master!' he called but the webbing held in his shriek. Even to draw a breath was an effort. The web held fast to his ankles and pulled at his hair. All this just to catalogue some dry old books that no one was ever going to read! He damned the books, damned the library, damned the city and all who lived in it. Looking up with wild eyes, he suddenly noticed a hole in the web. He struggled with difficulty on all fours and forced himself through it as if battling through a blizzard. Gradually the storm abated, he was back on his feet, the wind was dying down. He felt his heart beating hard as he ran the last fifty metres towards the light-bulb he now saw twinkling at him from the end of the tunnel.

The Du Traheus was poring over the books on the tiny desk, a bottle in one hand and two glasses in the other. He hardly looked up as Gregor burst from the tunnel of books and fell head first to the floor at his feet, followed by a swirling mass of dust and cobwebs.

'Drink?' offered the librarian. 'It's rather dusty down there, isn't it?'

Gregor grabbed the drink and gulped it down. 'Dusty?' he gasped. 'Have you been to where the nets close in?'

'I know every spider personally. They're big brutes too. Well, never mind, you obviously didn't meet one.'

Gregor shook his head. 'You've got quite a department here,' he said, brushing the cobwebs from his trousers.

The Du Traheus picked up one of the index-cards from Gregor's desk. 'What are these cards?' he asked turning it over in his hand. 'What exactly are you doing?'

'I'm cataloguing the department, sir. One card for every book, one box for every letter of the alphabet. I've already catalogued over five thousand volumes for you.'

'Memory is your best memo,' said the Du Traheus. 'Five thousand, you say?'

'Correct.'

'And you are twenty something?'

'Seven, sir.'

'Well, you'll need to live to be three hundred and fifteen to do them all, in that case.' He replaced the index-card on the table. 'I had better not hold you up.'

'Sir,' said Gregor as he squeezed himself behind his desk, 'is all the mythology in the world here?'

'No,' answered the Du Traheus. 'Only words are here. They try to make me yield the rest but my words come from the North Country. They can't be pinned down between book covers. Our words like to play on the breeze. They congregate in the hollows of streams and fill the ravines. The authorities don't like to think about things like that, now, do they? Could you recognize an adder stone? Do you understand that you're here to help me? Do you?'

'Well,' said Gregor, having understood very little, 'you're the boss.' He held back a yawn. The Du Traheus began lumbering back towards his pulpit. Gregor began leafing through one of the books on his desk. Five thousand in the bag, he thought. Only fifty-eight million or so to go if the Du Traheus was to be believed. There must be a better way to make a living. Cataloguing Mythology was such boring, repetitive work. Was that what all these books were about? He started reading about the fair people in caves who passed their days juggling golden balls and passed their nights wandering the countryside, seen only by children and old people. He saw three golden balls trickling from hand to hand and their colour flowing yellow in a black stream. He heard sharp little voices chirruping and laughing. Between tree-trunks of oak he could see their paths weaving across the floor of the forest, and among the moss covered stones that bubbled like green foam. He could hear a river rumbling. In the distance there was a bright gap where the woods seemed to end. As he got nearer he saw fields of pasture swelling under their lattice of walls. He went towards a plume of smoke which came, as he saw presently, from the stone chimney of a farm where hens scratched around the farmyard and ducks waddled. As he knocked, the door swung open creakily, its base was worn as if chewed by a dog. An old woman wearing a white lace cap and black clothes was ladling broth from a cauldron into the bowl held out by an old man with long grey hair. Gregor sat at the table and was given a bowlful of broth full of potatoes and carrots and swirling steam. A young girl came in, dressed like the old woman, and put two loaves of bread in the middle of the table. When Gregor asked about the fair people and their balls of gold the old man laughed and reached for a book on the dresser from which he read aloud. Gregor listened to the words flowing from his lips and watched them flutter like butterflies off the page and climb along the bars of the setting sun through the window. The pale blue plates on the dresser flushed orange as the shadows deepened. The words rose and flew, black like crows against the red sun. And as the sun sank into the branches of the trees the red eyes of the peat fire winked on the hearth and the glow softly hissed and the voice of the old man grew quiet. Gregor sensed a new presence close to him.

'Sleeping on the job, is it?' Adam Laban poked him spitefully. 'What's the matter with the bed at our place? Has a pea got under your mattress or something?'

'I dozed off, Adam. I'll work late to make up lost time...'

'The Du Traheus will pay for this,' said Adam Laban. 'And if it were not for mother sticking up for you, you'd be getting it in the neck and all.'

Gregor felt rather ashamed to have been caught out again. He reached for another book and started to browse through it but could not concentrate. The letters simply swam before his eyes as the words began lifting up off the paper one by one and circling around his head like mistle thrushes following one another around a tree. His eyelids were closing like shutters on shop windows. He found himself standing on a grassy plain with fields and dikes and woodlands all around. Above him a big sun beat down. It was so hot that every breath burnt his throat. Under-foot he could feel the earth was hard and dry. There was no wind or breeze moving through the brambles. From afar there came to him the voices of men, increasing gradually: voices shouting and laughing. The heat was in his nose and throat. He heard feet drumming on the hard earth. Then he saw them. Fifteen, perhaps twenty of them. Some in uniform, others wearing civilian clothes. Bayonets flashed in the sun, automatic rifles clanked against buckles; two men carried a band-saw which caught the glint of the sun. A young man was being frog-marched before the mob. His white shirt was open to the waist, his red neckerchief hung loose around his neck. He was trying to keep his balance as the soldiers shoved and kicked him from behind. Sunlight gleamed on bottles that were being passed from hand to hand. The youth stumbled once, then fell; he was grabbed roughly and given a shove that sent him sprawling. The men's voices were muffled by the heat. They were soon out of sight. Gregor stood where he was until he could once again hear the droning of insects above the beating of his own heart. He ventured after them. Something bright caught his eye. He bent to pick up a silver button that lay in the dirt. There was a rustling in the leaves. Perhaps a breeze was getting up. A cloud was preparing to slide across the sun. Was it only he who felt the earth stirring and rising and falling like waves on the sea? He felt his legs give under him and he tried to steady himself by grabbing at the dike but he was falling through the earth's skin with stones and soil flowing down on top of him. His stomach churned. His forehead gave a bang as it struck the desk.

The Du Traheus laughed. 'Up to no good again, I see,' he said, rubbing the side of his head. 'It's no wonder that Adam Laban is annoyed. What would he do if he knew that you were actually reading the books?'

'I'm sorry,' Gregor apologized. 'I must be tired. Did he hit you?'

'That's nothing new,' said the Du Traheus with a wry smile. 'But listen here, we won't have any books left the way you keep devouring them.'

'How do you mean, sir?'

'Just look,' said the librarian, gesturing towards the open book that Gregor had been reading. Gregor jumped to his feet. There was nothing left but plain white paper.

'The words!' said Gregor. 'Where did they go?'

'That's for you to find out,' said the Du Traheus, tapping his nose. 'But come, it can wait. I've got rather a nice plum brandy that I would like you to try.'

4

From her bedroom window she looks down over the laurels towards the harbour where boats are waiting for the tide. The writing paper in front of her glares blankly at her. Dear Gregor, she writes, in rounded letters. She wants to say she misses him, that she's lonely here without him. She wants to say she loves him. But sometimes these things are hard to say. So she tells him about her day-to-day things. She asks him to please write. He did promise. Had he been caught she would soon have heard about it; people were being sent back all the time. She knew he had got through, she just couldn't understand why she was still waiting for a word from him. She knew he had to go, eventually. More than anyone she had noticed how the world of a seaside town was confining him, pressing down upon his shoulders. Hadn't she even encouraged him to get on with the things he felt he had to do? She didn't care what he did: it was only his pride after all. His stupid pride kept pushing them apart. Maybe once he got wherever he was going he would see more clearly than he did at home. Or he might find once he'd climbed his mountain that there was nothing to be seen but clouds and mist. She didn't care, so long as he got himself sorted out. She would not mind whether they lived in a castle or a stable. Why had he not written? She raises her eyes again. The tide comes in so quickly. She watches a fishing boat move past the jetty on its way out to sea. Grey clouds hang low over the horizon. 'Alice, can you hear me?' Her mother's voice is calling from the foot of the stairs. She puts down her pen. 'Just coming, mother.' She glances at the letter she has just written. Scrunching the paper into a ball she tosses it onto the pile in her waste-paper bin under her desk by the window of her room.

53

'By the way,' said Gregor as they sipped the plum brandy, 'about the North Country.'

'What about it?' said the Du Traheus.

'Well, it's just I've heard a bit about the place. Isn't that where they dress up all old-fashioned like?'

'They do retain a certain attachment to their traditional garb,' said the Du Traheus. 'But the costumes are on the outside. What's more important are their ancient legends. It would be worth your while hearing their tales. There are only a few left who know them all.' He knocked the bowl of his pipe against his ashtray. A faraway look was clouding his eyes. Gregor imagined he was probably watching a cloud pass over the North Country.

'Is it important for these tales to be retained?' asked Gregor as he emptied the remains of the bottle into his glass. A variety of soft fruits fell down into the neck of the bottle causing several drops to splash out over the table. Whatever the Du Traheus used as an infusion in his brandy, it certainly gave it a strange taste.

'Of course it's important.' The Du Traheus glared at him. 'What else do you think we're doing here? Don't the authorities insist that we catalogue every last one of them? And I'm told we need to hurry too, before they've all been wiped out. They need the material for some museum, apparently.'

'Aren't you from the North Country yourself?' Gregor felt he needed to get things straight.

'Yes, among other places.' He drew a hand down his beard. 'I'm a storyteller. I don't mean to boast when I say I could beat the lot of them - except maybe Dail Coed, of course. And just look at me now, the keeper of books in a prison of words.'

'Do you regret stealing their words, then?'

The Du Traheus looked horrified. 'I stole nothing, Gregor. It was me that was stolen, not the words. Mabon does not come close to what I got, and as for that dim-witted Gwair, he doesn't know he was born. No one has got it worse than I have. Never was anyone so sorely chained. And do I spend every minute moaning about it? No, unlike Mabon and Co. I suffer my fate in silence. But here I shall remain, and all for the want of an adder stone. Of course the words came with me but they won't get them from me no matter how hard they try. And in the mean time, my North Country adder stone is far away.'

'I thought you were happy here,' said Gregor.

'What's that?' asked the Du Traheus.

'Well, you've always seemed quite contented down here in your underground shell, swigging brandy to your heart's content. Not everyone can live in the past, you know.'

'I'm not everyone,' said the Du Traheus defiantly. 'And this is not the past. Sometimes I can feel like I'm a hundred years ago and sometimes I feel a hundred years hence, even a thousand years. What difference does it make? It's a circle, like rain.'

'Oh, sure it is,' said Gregor raising his glass. 'Here's to the next thousand.' He drained his glass and picked up a book with a fine leather spine. He looked at the Du Traheus through the corner of his eye. 'Am I right in thinking that you need someone to bring you something from the North Country?'

'Who would be my messenger, Gregor? One with black plumage and a yellow beak, perhaps? Or a fleet messenger with neither feet nor wings? No, neither the blackbird nor the wind will help me this time. I'd be hard pressed to find anyone who'd be man enough for that job. Very bad it is, up North. It's a backward place at the best of times - got no use for technology, see. No machines, no television, just words. It's well I remember those hills thick with tourists; they were from the Capital States. Came down to see us with their cameras and their videos. They don't get many tourists in the North Country now. Who would go to a place like that, now it's all shot to hell?'

'Me, sir.'

'No one in their right mind would go there now,' said the Du Traheus firmly. 'Tourists are a timid breed, Gregor. They used to come a-plenty; like bloody locusts they were, in their air-conditioned coaches. They never seemed to talk to one another very much, maybe that was why they couldn't understand our language. They laughed at our words because they could not use them. When the trouble started they all buggered off back to their air-conditioned coaches. You won't find tourist traffic through the mountain tunnels nowadays, Gregor, or over the passes.'

Gregor coughed into his fist. 'If you want someone to record some fables for you in the North Country, I'm your man.'

'The North Country?' mused the Du Traheus relighting his pipe. 'Yes, I remember it well.' He sat back staring into space as if contemplating the geography of his mind.

'Excuse me, sir,' said Gregor.

'I know what you said, Mr Under-cataloguer,' said the Du Traheus, starting up and gripping the arm of his chair. 'Can't you see I'm busy?' He sank back into his chair. In due course his head began to droop until it sagged to his breast and his breathing turned to snoring. Gregor was already part way through another bottle. It looked like this was going to be a long night. Perhaps there was some more bread and cheese left. He got up to look. The Du Traheus opened his eyes and said, 'That will be all.'

'What?' said Gregor.

'You can go now.'

'But what about...?'

'Yes, you can go to the North Country.'

'I can?'

The Du Traheus got clumsily to his feet and struggled up his pulpit. 'I've got a licence for you somewhere here. Let's see your identity card.' He looked askance at it. 'Is that the best these cowboys can do nowadays?' He tossed it back to Gregor. 'How much does he charge for rubbish like that?'

Gregor told him. The Du Traheus laughed. 'Here,' he said throwing Gregor a new licence. 'Don't try crossing any borders with the plastic you got from the tramp.'

The new card was made of hard flat plastic, with his own photo embedded in it like a fly in amber. The words GREGOR MARINI: RECORDER OF FABLES. CITY LIBRARY were printed underneath 'Very impressive,' he said. 'Where did you get the photo? From the security camera?'

'You'll get more details later,' said the Du Traheus.

'Why don't I just write down some details now,' offered Gregor, taking an address book out of his jacket pocket. It came out between his finger and thumb and between its leaves lay a silver button round and clean. Gregor turned it over several times in his hand.

The Du Traheus shook his head. 'No.' he said

Gregor looked up. 'Do you think a tape-recorder might be useful?'

'It would not,' replied the Du Traheus. 'All you'd get would be an empty tape. You can't trap their words that easily. Come on, it's late. Go home.'

Gregor pocketed his notebook and the button and bid his master good-night.


He was only just blowing on his stew and putting some butter on his bread. A redheaded lad burst into the café. Gregor recognized him. Apparently he recognized Gregor too, because he was coming over towards him. He was the boy who had sent Gregor flying down the stairs.

'It's rather unthoughtful of you, Gregor,' said the boy.

'What is?'

'To stay out late like this, without rhyme or reason or going near your residence all day. I've had to scour the city looking for you. It's just not good enough. What right have you got to interrupt their schedule? The Office's messengers are busy enough as it is.' He sat down heavily at Gregor's side and reached over for the bread and butter.

Gregor decided to ignore this impudence. 'As it happens,' he said, 'I was in my room all afternoon.'

'I don't care tuppence for your excuses,' said the redhead. 'All I'll say to you is that you'd better go to your room at once. Even this is more than I should say. I'm doing it to get your co-operation. You'd better leave this food and go.' The redhead glanced up once or twice. He drew the stew towards him and dunked a piece of bread into it. The youth's appearance had stolen Gregor's appetite. He hoped the red boy would choke on his stew; Gregor didn't want it.

A shudder went through him as he pulled open the door to his room. He didn't like cold rooms. He sat on his bed to wait. He was tired and his eyes hurt. Finally he got up. He thought there might be a night-porter on duty. Someone who could tell him what it was all about.

The house grunted and groaned as it settled down for another cold night. A draught blew low along the long corridors.

He followed the steps higher into the house

On one of the upper floors a warm current of air suddenly stroked his cheek. He turned towards it. A little stairwell led off the main corridor downwards. At the foot of the stairwell the carpet hardly covered the wooden boards of the passage that led to a door framed with light. From within came laughter. He paused a moment. When he got closer he could see a tall thin man in a tail-coat talking with his back to the door. He kept shaking a piece of paper held in his hand. 'We'll call him up presently,' he said loud enough for Gregor to hear. The man then bent forward and Gregor saw a little crystal glass sparkle in his gloved hand. Firelight splayed from the glass straight into Gregor's eye. He shifted position and a board creaked underfoot.

The door flew open. 'This is an unexpected pleasure,' said the tall thin man. He pocketed his piece of paper. 'Eavesdropping, is it? Come in here so as I can see who you are... It's him. Better the man who came after a year than the man who never came, is it? I am sorry to disappoint you, sir, but you are rather late. Even the messengers have given up on you and gone to bed. This will not do.'

Unsure what to say, Gregor just stared. A log fire crackled in the grate. Adam Laban sat on a leather sofa by the fire. A black-haired, slender girl with dark eyes sat on his lap. They shared the sofa with Llygad Bwyd, his glass held heavily in his hand.

'Come in and shut the door,' shouted Adam Laban. 'I've got questions for you.'

Gregor looked about him.

'Come on in,' said the girl. 'And welcome.' The flames from the fire reflected on her bracelet. 'Sit down with me here for a while,' she said.

Gregor looked up at the tall thin man in the long coat. 'No,' said the tall man. He pointed to a hard chair. At least the fire was warm.

'Let me introduce you, Gregor,' said the girl, 'I'm Mwnwgl Wyn.' She raked her fingers through Adam Laban's matted hair. 'And of course, you know Adam, don't you ?' She looked up at the tall man. 'And this is Sebedeus,' she said with a sweep of the arm.

The man made a contemptuous bow towards Gregor and said nothing. Mwnwgl Wyn turned towards the tramp. 'And this is Llygad Bwyd.'

'How are you, Llygad Bwyd?' asked Gregor.

'I don't know you,' said Llygad Bwyd.

'Oh, I see.' Gregor put his hands in his pockets. 'Well,' he said 'If I'm late, I'm sorry. The message was to wait in my room.' He noticed Sebedeus give Adam Laban a searching glance. 'So I waited. I look for somebody in authority. Obviously it was the messenger who made the mistake, not me.'

Sebedeus continued to stare coldly at Adam Laban.

'Oh, you're clever!' snarled Adam, lifting Mwnwgl Wyn off his knee. He walked up to Gregor and put his arms either side of him on the arms of the chair. His sour breath engulfed Gregor. 'How dare you insinuate that a messenger representing this house got his message wrong? When Mam hears of this, she will see through you. I'll call for Cochyn Messenger rightaway so that we can have proof of your lies.'

'We need not disturb the red-headed one tonight, Adam,' said Sebedeus carefully. 'The insinuation is preposterous. It would be a stain on a white steed to give half an ear to such ridiculous nonsense. He tries to pass the blame as if it were a parcel. But I'm afraid he'll find you can't do that in this country.'

'Thanks, Sebedeus.' Adam Laban got up. 'Mam and I are grateful for your confidence.' He walked up to Gregor. 'You'll pay for this,' he snarled.

'He's a stranger,' said Mwnwgl Wyn. 'He didn't understand. Don't be so hard on him, Adam. We should not fight like this. He can see the messengers tomorrow. In the mean time he's our guest.' She turned to Gregor. 'Come on now, take a glass-ful with us, Gregor. Come closer to the fire.'

Gregor didn't refuse the glass he was offered. 'If I've messed up your plans then I'm sorry. I didn't do it voluntarily but out of unfamiliarity.'

'Unfamiliarity?' asked Llygad Bwyd.

'Yes,' said Adam Laban. 'He has plenty of that and....'

'Mwnwgl Wyn is right,' broke in Sebedeus. 'Nothing can be achieved tonight in discussing his case. For once the Office messengers are prepared to come back in the morning. I'd say Gregor owes Mrs Laban gratitude in arranging for them to wait. But Gregor, make sure you appear before the Office messengers tomorrow morning ?'

'Yes, that's fine by me,' said Gregor nodding amiably towards the company trying to decide if he should ask where and when. He placed his empty glass on the table. 'Well, if that's all, and with your permission, I'm off to get some sleep before the interview.'

'At last,' growled Adam Laban. 'Now give me your identity card.' Gregor passed him the card he had bought from Llygad Bwyd. 'You'll get this back in the morning,' smiled Adam Laban, taking the card. He turned to Llygad Bwyd. 'You used to be so good with these cards,' he said. 'This is shoddy.'

Just before dawn the following morning there was a commotion at Gregor's door. Adam Laban stood on the landing pounding the door with his fists and shouting.

'Get out of bed, you maggot!' he screamed. 'Come on, wake up! You're late again, you arsehole, get out of bed!'

Mrs Laban, with arms folded, stood in her dressing-gown behind her son.

'Why don't you just give me the key, Mam?' pleaded Adam. 'Why spoil a good door ?'

He turned the key in the lock.

A cold morning met them through the window. The curtains waved briskly at them in the breeze, like a hanky from a train window. Paperweighted by some coins on the table was a note and some paper money. Adam rushed to the bed and turned it over. He ripped open the wardrobe while his mother read the note. Adam stuck his head out of the window as she pocketed Gregor's remittance.

'Adam,' said his mother when he finally climbed down swearing uglily from the window, 'I don't ever want to hear you using that word again, do you understand?'

'Sorry, Mam,' said Adam.

Sebedeus came into the room. 'What happened?' he said.

Adam pointed to the window.

Sebedeus put his head out. He brought it back in again and shook it.

'What is he, a fly?' demanded Adam.

'Well, he's not here, is he?' said Sebedeus.

'We were watching the door all night, weren't we, Mam?' said Adam. 'And anyway, I know where he'll be. I'll catch him!' He began to chew on his left knuckle. 'I'll kill him for this ...'

'Adam!' warned Mrs Laban.

Sebedeus pointed his finger at Adam. 'If you don't get him back you know what will happen.' His upper lip rose in distaste.

'I'm not worried.' Adam Laban's face was taut as a greyhound's. 'I want him too.' He pushed past them and ran downstairs. Some moments later the whole house shook under the weight of the slam that he gave to the door.

'Goodmorning, Adam,' said the Du Traheus. He put down his quill pen and pushed his spectacles to the end of his nose.

'Where is he?' Adam looked quickly about him.

'Who exactly, Adam?' asked the Du Traheus. He got out a piece of blotting-paper to dry his nib.

'Don't you start,' screamed Adam Laban. 'That snake Gregor? When I've sorted him you'll suffer for this.' He threw some chairs and table to one side.

Adam dragged the Du Traheus by the beard to Gregor's desk. 'Are you going to deny it now, you bearded baboon?' He pointed to Gregor's footprints slinking off into the distance. 'Wanted to protect your protégé. Is that it? You're going to be sorry. But first we get your boy.'

'Adam!' shouted the Du Traheus after him, 'he was never my protégé. Why would I wish to protect him? All he did was mess around and play tricks and get in my way. The guilty flees with nobody chasing him, they say. Just follow his footsteps. There's no escape.'

The Du Traheus could hear his muttering get fainter as he followed Gregor's footsteps away from the pool of light. The Du Traheus scratched his head for a moment. The sounds faded into silence. He cupped his hands to his mouth. 'Oh, by the way, Adam!' he called. 'Adam, be careful of the spiders.' He peered down one of the tunnels of books but there was nothing. 'Adam!' he shouted again. He was quite hoarse from shouting and needed a drink. Anyway, they had not been fed for ages, poor huge greedy things. He pulled the cord that worked the light bulb above Gregor's desk.

A light burned above the pulpit. He got out a bottle of sloe gin. As he opened it the thread of a voice came across the acres of books, like the remains of a scream.

He raised his glass. 'Good hunting, Gregor.'

5

The heat shimmers like a hawk over the stubble. The air is close and damp like the breath of a dog. Between the sharp cut stems, the soil sweats around her. Cushions of bracken lie on the dikes under willow branches. His waistcoat lies on the ground. She grabs it. One button is missing. On the hot breeze, distant voices shout across the fields. A blur of colour moves behind willow branches. Sunlight glints on metal. There is drunken laughter and glass breaking. Heads are bent over their task. Across the fields she wants his blue eyes to find her eyes again. But their eyes cannot connect. Rough hands are forcing his neck down under the bandsaw. The great teeth come down and bite into his white skin. He raises a hand to grab at nothing. His cry is frozen on his lips. The laughter has stopped. The afternoon is dead. She listens to his name beating in her heart. The world is quiet now. Leaves fail to stir. No birds circle slowly in the wide sky. She falls to her knees among the cigarette-ends and broken bottles and gathers the congealing blood from the sticky grass. Nothing else remains. On her knees with the blood in her hands she sucks it from her salty fingers. Insects struggle in the pools of blood and on her fingers and in her hair. When she rises, the shadows are already falling along the dikes and midges are dancing among the early stars. Her white lace cap lies where it has fallen. She gathers up his waistcoat in her arms.

The tram rumbled and clanked along its silver rails. A thin mist was curling around the street-corners. Gregor picked bits of paint and plaster from his clothes. The bruised dawn was spreading all around them. Occasionally the sun threatened to break through the clouds. He was thinking about the black drainpipe and the backyard wall. If nothing else he'd have a good story to tell back home. Whenever that might be. A crack was appearing in the eastern sky. The sun's fingertips probed through and snatched a sudden flame from a line of puddles. A tide of rubbish rolled around under his seat. The tram was cheap enough, he supposed: too cheap to bother with a heating system, obviously. When the Tannoy announced his stop he dragged his bag off the rack. After the rolling tram the pavement seemed hard and unyielding. Spats of rain speckled his jacket and his hair. Clouds of white steam rolled out from long black grilles along the walls. Men in white coats were hurrying here and there, their aprons spattered red. On their shoulders they heaved split pigs with their skin still steaming. Apparently the station was next to the slaughterhouse district. An oily, fatty smell filled the air. Here and there the yellow lights of cafés broke the shadows. Some squealing pigs were dragged past. From behind a wall he heard the deep lowing of cattle. The cobbled street shone after the shower, making the pools of blood stand out darker than the stones. He stepped carefully to avoid the pools as he crossed over to the main entrance. The northern line station was housed in a huge, oblong dusty building with windows so grimy that the light from inside was not visible from without. As he pushed the door open he was met by a gush of warm stale air. Why did every railway station smell like this? On the walls were pasted huge paper timetables. He tried to make sense of the tiny lines of print.

Giving up on the timetables, he joined a queue. The person in front of him seemed to be discussing a fabulously complicated itinerary with the clerk in a language neither understood. As Gregor was deciding to join a different queue the person in front moved away. A green light indicated that it was his turn. He walked up and spoke into the microphone.

'What?' asked the clerk. His head and shoulders could vaguely be seen moving to and fro inside his cage.

'As far as she goes,' repeated Gregor into the mouthpiece. 'North.'

The clerk bent towards the grill. 'North, you say?'

'Is there a problem?'

The clerk laughed. 'Been there before, have you?'

'Yes,' lied Gregor.

'Place your travel documents in the tray.'

Gregor placed his library card into the trough.

'Okay,' confirmed the Clerk. 'North it is then. All the way. That'll be seven hundred million five hundred thousand and ten in local currency or seven dollars if you're paying with foreign notes.'

Gregor placed a ten-dollar bill in the tray.

When it opened again his ticket and library card lay in it. 'What about my change?' demanded Gregor.

'You said you'd been before,' said the Clerk pressing the green light.

'Yes, but...'

'So you know what happened to the change.' The next customer was trying to jostle past Gregor. 'Now get a move on or you'll miss it,' hissed the clerk.


As the train pulled out of the station it had to wait for a string of livestock waggons to cross the points. Calves thrust out their damp noses. The steam of their breath reminded Gregor of the pigs' bodies he'd seen on men's shoulders by the slaughterhouses. He caught the gaze of one round uncomprehending eye staring at him intently between the bars. He had heard that people were once transported in waggons like these. Perhaps they were the very same waggons. He watched the eye draw away from him slowly and then disappear as the waggon wound out of sight towards the railtrack holding pens.

The train moved forward. The electricity poles were picking up speed. They were rolling like the picture on a faulty television set until they finally blurred and blended together. Soon the landscape opened beyond the city. Houses and streets fell away. The train's nose was burrowing into a world of fields and farmyards, country lanes and trees.

'Travel documents!' The soldier shouted in the vernacular. He stood at the head of the carriage, an automatic weapon slung over one shoulder. His boots were very black. He repeated the command in an international language. 'Messieurs, Mesdames, vos passeports, s'il vous plait.'

He stood at Gregor's shoulder. 'Monsieur?'

'Good morning.'

'Oh, you're a local,' said the soldier. 'Got your documents?'

'Of course.' Gregor handed him his library card.

'OK,' said the soldier. He handed Gregor back his card. 'From the library, is it?' He looked at Gregor again. 'Won't pay their fines up there in the North Country?' He laughed as soldiers sometimes laugh. 'Or are you going to teach them how to read and write? Is that your purpose, Librarian?'

Gregor affected a grin.'Something like that,' he mumbled

Gregor raised his head slowly as the soldier swaggered down the carriage away from him. The butt of his gun was banging on the backs of seats but nobody turned.


Gregor began watching the morning stream past the window. His eyes would follow hedges and feel the contours of the fields. Wood pigeons fled from the branches of an old alder tree. A horse and cart stood waiting at a crossing. Perhaps they were on their way to the mill, or to the market. There was fresh mud on the horse's fetlocks; the spokes of the wheel were crusted with mud and the rims glistened. In the front seat sat a mute, unflinching couple: man and wife probably. In the back a figure slouched as if sleeping. The couple's upturned eyes fell on him; he could feel their gaze. The farmer in his soft felt hat. The farmer's wife under white lace headgear. He was thinking about his grey face in the window of a train. Do they know that I am? Could he ever know where they were going that morning or how they lived ? This train was not in their morning or in their world. It was passing them by as it passed them by always. Until you arrive you can never stop travelling. Gregor imagined their eyes meeting his. He wanted to spit on their settled reality. They would never need to catch a train. He looked into the sky to try to wipe out their stare. If there were mountains up there behind the clouds no one would have known about it today. If it never stops raining how do they tell the height of the mountains? Lower down they passed farms with backyards running right to the line. Sometimes a yellow kitchen light. Upstairs lights and people moving. What happiness, what heartbreak was moving between these people at the break of day? A woman stood on her kitchen doorstep casting grain. The hens pecked at it like the toy he had once owned. They pecked and pecked at the grain as a wooden ball turned and turned beneath them to make them peck.

But as if watching a movie for the second time Gregor got bored. The view was fine as views go but other images began to move among his thoughts. It was warm, the rhythmic thrashing of the wheels lulled him. He started when he heard the gulls screech above the streets of his hometown. He saw Alice standing on the porch. A ray of sun shone on her face and made her look sad. She must have known that he could not hang around indefinitely waiting for any old something to turn up. Then he had lost his job. They had discussed things. There were opportunities abroad, he would get on fine, and do a lot better than he had in his own country! Anyway, maybe their time apart would give them the opportunity to evaluate their relationship and maybe begin to map out a future together. He knew it did not sound very romantic. But the town was just getting on his nerves, it was too restricting, even the grey skies oppressed him. He had to go anyway, even if it were simply to show he could stand on his own two feet. As he had begun to warm to his theme he had paused for breath and only then had he noticed the teardrop in her eye. 'Alice, please don't,' he had said.

How easy his plans had seemed then as he looked to the future. How confident he had been as he bade her farewell. They stood on the steps and sunlight played through her hair. The green air smelt of wet laurel leaves and pine. From the harbour came a hint of salt on the breeze.

'Excuse me, is this seat taken?'

Gregor woke up. He noticed her rather crumpled white cap. Then her calloused hands. 'No, it's not taken,' said Gregor. He had not noticed the train stopping anywhere.

She wedged her packs on the luggage-rack above his head and sat opposite. 'It's cold outside,' she said. 'There is snow in it, mark my words.'

'If you say so.'

'Going far, then, are you?'

'North,' said Gregor. She seemed to be a talkative one. 'Are you from this area?' he asked politely.

'Why else would I be here?' She unwrapped a lump of bread from some grey paper. 'You're a journalist, then?' she asked. She offered Gregor a piece of bread.

Gregor declined. 'What makes you say that?'

'Why else would you be going North? You're like vultures you lot are.' She pushed a hunk of bread into her mouth and turned her face towards the window. 'See what I say,' said she after some chewing and swallowing. 'Snowing already.'

The snowflakes whirled about like sparks from a bonfire. Gregor went in search of the refreshments counter. They seemed a very talkative lot He was beginning to feel almost at home. Even the soldier had thought he was local.

Sunk back into his seat he drained off some beer from his bottle. No, she explained, she was not from the North Country. He chewed on a handful of salted peanuts. She was from the hill country. Been down the plains selling salt pork, butter, pickles. North Country people? Of course she knew them. She knew them even though she wasn't one of them. She bent forwards and touched a thick finger to her lace cap. 'Why do I wear it?' she asked. 'Tradition, is it? No, force of habit. We've forgotten why we wear these ornaments. In the North Country they wear these things every day. It's not just a white cap they put on up there, they wear a whole costume and they say every stitch has some significance. They hold fast to the old ways. It's their belief, you know. Some say they even keep the old gods. That's what the husband says. He knows more than me about them, but he doesn't talk very much. He won't be going amongst them now. What with the troubles. They don't like worldly goods up there in the North Country so there's not much trade for trinkets. They call it their White Land of Hills. That's their name for the place, you know that? Strange name for a cold damp bleak place where it never stops raining. And that's all I know about the place. More than enough to put in your newspaper, probably.'

'I don't work for a newspaper...'

'So you're with a film crew? Well you might as well not bother. You won't get pictures of them - they don't believe in it.'

'Look,' said Gregor firmly, 'I only work for the library.' He finished his beer. The train stopped at a station, people got off. It was getting dark. When they pulled beyond the lights the few passengers left were reflected in the windows. Gregor could not decide whether the train felt faster or slower when it seemed to be going through a tunnel. Faster, probably, he thought.

Eventually the woman got up. 'Well,' she said gesturing towards her things. 'Nearly there'.

Gregor got up to help her down with her bags.'Getting off at the next stop?'

'So will you be, son,' she advised. 'Last stop.'

'But I've got a ticket for the North Country,' protested Gregor.

She took his ticket in her hand. 'You've been taken for a

ride. Ain't no trains heading north. Ain't nothing going north but trouble.'

'The swine took a three-dollar tip from me.'

'They saw you coming way off.' She gestured at her baggage and beckoned Gregor to follow her. 'You take care with those bags now,' she scolded as he struggled towards the door. 'Come on, I'll get you on your way,' she said. The train's wheels were grinding down. Gregor got her things to the door and fetched his own bag. Station lights were passing, there were a few figures on the white platform.

A crust had formed on the ground, fine feathers of snow swarmed around the lights. No one got onto the train. The driver and the guard met on the platform, shook hands and crossed to the station building. Perhaps the soldier had got off lower down the line.

She showed him where to stow her luggage. He was pushing them up onto some shelves in a darkened hall. She said she had business to attend to. She was sure the Station-master would help. Why didn't he go through to the café to wait? She would try to find the Station-master, maybe have a word with him. See what could be arranged. She pointed to a door with yellow light seeping through fine cracks. He pulled the door towards him.

Across one corner of the railway café ran the serving counter; half a dozen tables filled the floor. Some men sat at one of the tables playing cards. Above them hung a fug of smoke. It was hot inside after the icy platform but none of these men had taken off their coats. Some even had scarves around their necks. Gregor's cheeks tingled in the warmth. Evidently most of the heat came from an iron stove with a long black pipe. There were only sweets and a few newspapers on the counter. Behind it on turquoise shelves dusty bottles full with coloured brandies.

'Have you got some soup?' Gregor asked the girl who came through from the back. 'Some bread and butter would be nice as well, and a bottle of beer if you've got one, please.'

'Okay,' she replied. 'How about a copy of *Papur Pawb*? Your picture is in it.'

'No it isn't.'

But it was: on page two under the heading Collector of Stories. Where the hell did they get that photo? It was not much of a story either. 'In the City Library yesterday, the trainee Under-cataloguer Gregor Marini was promoted to the position of Collector of Stories.'

Gregor took his beer and went to a table by the stove to check the paper again. His soup came, and his bread and butter and cold beer. The soup was hot and had lumps of meat in it. And no red messenger was going to be stealing his food tonight.

Gregor glanced up from his food when the driver and the guard came in. The smell of oil forced him to notice them. He saw them sit down at a table in the middle of the room. Almost as they sat the girl produced two platefuls of roast meat and gravy and roast potatoes and then a loaf of bread, some butter and wine. Gregor looked back in disbelief into his now empty soup bowl. There was one small piece of potato left which he lifted on the tip of his spoon.

A mighty roar of laughter came from the card players' table. There was much slapping of cards on the table and scraping of chair-legs on the slate floor. The occasional 'Nos dawch, Lleucu,' rang out amidst slapping of shoulders. As they filed out, a gulp of cold air flew into the room. Gregor shuddered. Lleucu came and took his bowl. Once she had cleared away the railwaymen's supper she began moving the furniture. The two rail-workers were still sprawled in their chairs. She motioned to them to get up. What the hell are they up to now? thought Gregor as he watched them lumber over to some cupboards at the end of the room and bring from it iron bed-frames, sheets and blankets. The next thing he knew they were getting undressed. Under their overalls they wore red and white stripey pyjamas. Soon they were sighing peacefully in their beds in the middle of the floor. What a primitive place, thought Gregor.

The girl was back behind the counter. Gregor felt sure those two had taken the last two beds available. He was quite obviously a second-class citizen in their eyes. It was warm. His head was drooping to his chest.

'Tickets, please!'

Gregor sat bolt upright.

A rotund man in a shiny peaked cap stood at the door. He had a silver chain hanging in a loop from his breast pocket. Gregor assumed he was the Station-master. He had a ticket punch in his hand. 'Tickets, please,' he repeated.

Gregor rummaged through his pockets. 'I've got it somewhere,' he explained.

'H'm,' said the Station-master sceptically.

Gregor found the ticket in his shirt pocket.

'That's better,' said the Station-master, breathing out as he punched Gregor's ticket. 'May I introduce my wife?'

'Your room is ready, Gregor,' said a strong, wide lady with a kindly face who came through from the kitchen as the Station-master was speaking. 'The maid will show you up.'

'Lleucu!' she called.

The shouting had no effect upon the two snorers in the middle of the floor.

The girl came in.

'Lleucu,' said the Station-master's wife, ' please show the gentleman up to his room.'

'Where is he, mistress?'

'Lleucu has only just started with us,' explained the wife of the Station-master.

'No problem,' said Gregor. 'I'm very grateful. I am a bit tired...'

'Come on then,' said Lleucu catching hold of his hand. 'You don't want to wake up Iron Man or Morus's brother, do you? Isn't it enough that you've taken their room?'

'I did no such thing!'

'Don't take any notice,' said the Station-master's wife. 'They're quite used to sleeping in strange places. I think they were probably thankful to be allowed to sleep so near to their machine. The closer they are, the better they dream.'

'Yes,' announced the Station-master. 'And Sionyn Troliau will be here at eight. He'll take you up to Tafarn-y-Bwlch.'

'What?' asked Gregor.

'Well didn't you arrange it just now with Shanw Troliau?' The Station-master looked searchingly at Gregor. 'You are going North, aren't you?'

Gregor followed the maid to the top of the stairs and down along the landing. She held his hand fast in the darkness. A candle would have blown out in the draughts that crossed the passage. In the room there was a red fire in the grate of glowing coals. The ceiling reflected the whiteness of the snow outside. There were two big comfortable-looking beds. 'There's your bed,' said Lleucu pointing. Gregor put down his leather bag. Light from the coals danced together around the room. Beyond the panes, feathers of snow floated down. He was waiting for Lleucu to go so he could get into bed. She just seemed to be pushing a poker into the fire. She got up and stood with her back towards Gregor. Black smoke trickled up the chimney. He suddenly realised she was getting undressed. He turned towards his own bed. He heard the springs give as she got into the spare bed. 'Good-night,' she called.

'Good-night,' said Gregor, getting into his bed. He put a hand to his cheek. Very strange, he thought. Mind you, he had no objections. Made the room smell nice. Very down to earth people. Very open, probably. Close to the earth. Why did people automatically assume that a boy and a girl sharing a room led to other things? There was obviously nothing farther from Lleucu's thoughts. She was just a natural country girl taking advantage of the chance to sleep the night in a warm bed. He turned over to feel the cold pillow on his burning cheek. The mattress squeaked as he moved.

'Well?' said Lleucu's voice from the other bed.

'Well what?'

'Well, are you coming over here to keep my feet warm or not?'

6

The Du Traheus slowly draws his finger across the manuscript in front of him. *Alder, Birch, Cedar, Dogrose. Seventy-two, four hundred and thirty-two, two thousand and eighty.* Slowly he builds the circles of the stars. The words and the numbers flow through him drawing him far away from this place to a high escarpment jutting out above the trees. Blue plumes of mist rise from the forest canopy. *Elm, Fir, Gorse, Hazel.* The sun's eye stares down at him. No birds sing, there is no breeze. The sun is still and naked. A black shadow now begins to gnaw at its perfect circumference. The black tortoise crawls across its face, defiling it. *Look to the face of your sun, sons of men and gods, and know that the children of Donn have lost the thunder and the lightning and the brightness that breaks the night. See how the firmament darkens and the stars and planets whirl in disorder. How came it to pass that the serpent swallowed the stone? Look, you gods of straw, upon the spirit which came among you and hear how it reproaches you: 'See me, for mine is the fire in the eye of Lleu; mine is the bright stone in the forehead of day. Mine are the serpents' fangs that dribble on your lands and bring forth your harvests.'* And even as the spirit rages there comes through the mist the mighty arms and shoulders of Gofannon and from his hand flies the lance of iron, steel and copper which transfixes the serpent-tortoise and rends it until it disgorges the light that it has swallowed. The blinding flash signals the rebirth of light bringing new gods into the world. *As the shadow moves from the face of the sun, a flame is kindled that will cause your conquerors to fall and will allow the stars and planets back to their rightful orbits.*

*The Du Traheus stands upon the high escarpment, his shadow
solidifying. In his left hand a heavy viper twitches in death and in
his right hand he holds aloft a round stone with a blue eye from
which the sun's rays shine. Ivy, larch, maple, oak. He flings the snake
into the abyss. He places the stone to his forehead. Poplar, rowan,
sycamore and thorn. Eyes closed he sits cross-legged. He is waiting for
the signal to board the vessel that will carry him between the islands
and the stars. The stone grows cold and brittle like an eggshell.
When he touches it between delicate fingers he feels nothing but
grains of sand. He knows now that time's ferry has not come. He
knows as he opens his eyes that his book-lined prison will again
envelop him. The manuscript lies open in front of him, its pages
covered in a fine layer of grit.*

The snow remained in the hollows but its smell was still
heavy on the breeze. Gregor was not refreshed by his night at the
railway station. Occasionally he would doze off despite the cold,
to be awoken almost immediately by the lurching of the buggy.
The tired-looking pony went so slowly up the hill that
pedestrians could have passed them but no-one did. The people
on the road were streaming downhill towards them in an
unbroken line. Gregor might have walked but water gushing
down the road dissuaded him. He felt a dull gnawing at his
bones and his feet were chilled through. He peered up at the
jagged precipices that overhung the road; high above him he
watched a black speck as it wheeled and turned; he heard a
raven's caw falling from its perch of cloud. Gregor pulled his coat
tighter about him and tried kicking his soles against the foot-
boards. The driver looked at him sarcastically. Sionyn Troliau was
a big, sallow man with a huge greatcoat tied about him like a
haystack. His pudding face protruded from a Balaclava helmet.
His breathing, like the breathing of his pony, came out in great
white clouds from his nose and mouth.

Still no one passed them. Occasionally, a cart loaded down
with people and furniture would squeeze past going down.
Mostly people walked, tripping over the ones in front, their feet

wrapped in cloths that sometimes dragged behind them in the mud. The women had scarves wrapped about their heads so that only their eyes could be seen. Their eyes seemed glazed like the eyes of fish on a marble slab.

The road was a zigzag of hairpin bends rising between great boulders left by ancient glaciers or some disgruntled giant. The road surface was smooth with markings painted on it in white and yellow - directions for some long-forgotten motor vehicles. Rusty road-signs held distances ridiculously large compared to the pace at which they were travelling. Mist and rain had merged together. Only the reeds glistened. A late morning was turning into an early dusk. Strange, he thought, how the whine of the wind gets louder and closer as the light fades. The wheels squelched, the pony's hooves clip-clopped; it no longer swished its tail when the whip stung its side. White streams veined the high pastures. Brooks gurgled across stones. The sound of bubbling water surrounded them, like the sound of bilge water slapping about in the bottom of a boat: the same creaking of boards, the same swirling of water. Men shouting and passing buckets as they try to bail her out but she still sinks steadily, inch by inch. Gregor woke up with a start next to Sionyn Troliau on the side of a mountain on the North Country marches.

Sionyn Troliau gave his pony another stinging bite with the whip. Brutal man, thought Gregor. He was probably lucky that the man did not speak to him. He had nothing to say to such a brute. Maybe the man had a speech impediment. For all Gregor knew, he might not even have a tongue. Gregor didn't care. All he wanted right now was to reach a warm place and get some food.

When would that be? The farther they travelled towards the North Country the slower the journey became. This was not how things were supposed to turn out. Especially after the good start he had made. He'd had no problems to begin with, Petrog Spalpin getting him a place on the boat and then the escape over the fence. The money he'd paid for the ticket would be no good to Petrog now. They'd probably confiscated it all when they caught him. He was probably back where he had started by now. Everyone could not hope to make it over, Gregor had just been lucky - not something that seemed to happen to him very often. He clenched his teeth, adjusted the position of the bag on his knees and began to study the grime under his fingernails. Nothing was going to stand between him now and the Capital States. He looked up as he felt the light changing.

The jagged rocks were burnished gold and the rushes were turned to silver. The road in front was a river of milk and the pedestrians' scarves were red and yellow and all the colours of the rainbow, and their eyes were bright. He turned around in time to see the breach in the cloud closing and the white sun taking its eye from the keyhole of day. When he turned back the world was grey again as drops of darkness fell around him like ink into water. Lights flickered weakly from somewhere high above the road. Could the pass possibly be so far? Water splashed and swilled with a growing intensity and the wind grew shriller still. Why should he feel uneasy? He was not part of their world. He was just passing through. He would mind his own business and keep his tongue to lick his own wounds. What would Alice say if she could see him now? She would laugh at him and call him a fool. And last night? Yes, well, last night didn't add up to much, did it? She didn't need to know about it, so who would be any the wiser? His future was more important than last night. They would all eat their words when he succeeded. He tried to convince himself by turning old words in his mind, "no matter how long the road or never ending the mountain from Cwm Mawddwy to Trawsfynydd, wherever a lad's heart is set, the upward climb will seem all downhill". Old verses were fine but this was the real world and he was pissed off. The talk of riches in the city. It was all just a con and he could see that now. But the tales about the Capital States must be true. Why on earth had their ship sailed straight into the harbour anyway? It was no bloody wonder everyone was sent back. All the time he'd been in the city he hadn't seen anyone from the ship. There was deep water running under the ground, deals unseen. One ship gets turned back to allow three more to slip in at a provincial harbour. They should have weighed anchor far out in the bay and taken boats across to some deserted beach. But there were stories of boats sinking or being sunk before ever reaching land.

Snowflakes were now falling. They seemed to be turning off the road.

Dark crosses divided the bright windows into panes. He assumed this was Tafarn-y-Bwlch. The pain in his backbone had become unbearable after hours crouched on the hard seat; it was good to get down and stretch his legs. Feathers of snow spiralled out of a black sky and burnt the skin of his face. He thought of May mornings thick with bluebells and green leaves but they seemed unimaginably far away. What did any of it matter anyway? Maybe it was not the fault of the weather that he was so cold. Sometimes even storms can be full of laughter. He regretted getting mixed up in all this. What did he know about refugees? Wasn't that what he had been? It wasn't his doing and it wasn't his world. The snow buzzed like a swarm of bees around the outside lights as they crunched over the yard to the front door.

'The bar is in there.' said Sionyn Troliau. There was nothing wrong with his voice. 'I've got business to attend to.'

Gregor followed his gesture.

Yellow light escaped from a door at the side of the passage.

Gregor pulled the door towards him and felt a wet wave of warmth break over him. He had to blink repeatedly to stop his eyes smarting. A sea of sound engulfed him.

'Shut the bloody door!' shouted a loud voice from the middle of the din.

Gregor closed the door. He was standing with his back to the door surveying the room when he felt a tugging at his sleeve.

'Petrog! Is it you?'

'No, it's my shadow,' said Petrog dryly.

'What's with the beard?'

Petrog wiped some froth from the black spongy mass that obscured his face. 'Do you like it?' He held out his hand. Gregor squeezed it. Petrog turned to his neighbour on the bench. 'Shift up, make room for a friend of mine.'

Gregor squeezed next to Petrog on the bench. A waitress wearing black with a white apron approached and stood waiting. 'Yes?' she shouted above the din.

There were several waitresses all dressed the same. They moved deftly between the tables, carrying platefuls of food on trays. Others carried large glass tankards full of frothy black beer.

The waitress shrugged and turned to go. 'He'll have meat stew, black beer and bring a bottle of brandy,' said Petrog half rising. 'And give me another of these.'

'Well,' said Petrog, watching Gregor finish his meal. 'Who'd have thought it possible?'

Gregor was wiping his plate with a hunk of bread. 'What?'

'Who else, I ask you?'

'What?' said Gregor getting annoyed.

'Who the hell else would try to cross the pass northwards when everyone else is going south? Aren't you ever the contrary one?'

'What about you?' Gregor complained. 'You weren't so sure of touch this time, were you? It was you they caught, remember, not me!'

'Oh, yes, I remember,' said Petrog. 'So what? So I got a lift downtown and a night in a cell. Do you think the city police were men enough to hold me long? Wasn't I out of there and on my way North in a day or so? I worked more tricks than a clown in a circus, greased a few palms and out I came. No one holds Petrog Spalpin down for very long.' He arched his back against the partition and stretched his legs under the table.

'So we'll travel North together then, shall we ?'

Petrog's eyes narrowed. 'Been there, done that,' he said. 'There's nothing left now.'

'You can't have been there very long.'

'Long enough,' said Petrog with a wry smile. 'What a waste of a nice place,' he added. 'Anyway, I made some contacts, did a few deals - there's still trade to be done in some areas - so I won't be going back empty-handed, after all.'

'Back?' Gregor put down his empty beer glass. 'What about the Capital States? We'll find gold there ?'

'Oh, sure,' sneered Petrog. 'And all the roads closed under the mountains.'

'There must be some way through,' Gregor persisted. 'I'm not going back. Nothing to go back to.'

'I see,' said Petrog knowingly. 'And there was I under the impression that you had quite a lot to go back to.'

'Well I haven't,' snapped Gregor. 'I can't go back without accomplishing something. I'm not going to turn back now. And my relationship with Alice is nothing to do with you.'

'That's true,' Petrog poured out two brandies.

A man knocked Petrog's elbow, making him spill some of the brandy on the table. 'Hey, quit shoving,' snarled Petrog.

'Anyway, if you must know,' continued Gregor picking up his glass and swallowing a mouthful, 'things could be better between us. It's my fault, probably. I know it is. It's just that I'm not quite ready, you know, to 'start living' as they say. I don't understand what they mean anyway. I mean, bloody hell, I've never been anywhere or done anything so how can I... and I don't even know what I want...'

'I understand,' said Petrog. 'So you've met someone else, is that it? Does she have a name or do I have to guess?'

Gregor looked shocked. 'There is nobody else... Don't be stupid. Anyway, I didn't catch her name. It was nothing. It's just the small things aren't right...'

Petrog laughed. 'You and your pride - someday you'll learn to swallow it. Are you going to tell me about it now?'

'About what, Spalpin? And it's not pride. It's self-respect.' Gregor drained his glass. 'I'd be like a fly in resin if I'd have stayed.'

Petrog smiled. 'The flies are still there long after the trees are all gone.'

'I'm not a fly. And I'm not a saint. I don't know why I'm telling you anything, Job's comforter. It was a one-night thing, at a railway station. She was friendly, it was cold...'

'I didn't ask anything,' said Petrog. 'Best of luck to you is all I say.' He shared out what was left in the bottle. They struck glasses.

'I suppose you're still just mucking around with the girls that you meet ?' Gregor said. 'You just use people.'

'No I don't,' protested Petrog. 'I do not "muck around". You've got to be very careful when there are so many involved. They'd fight amongst themselves if I showed any one of them special favours.'

'That's a load of crap,' said Gregor with a laugh. 'But seriously, shouldn't you be thinking about making a nest for yourself pretty soon? You don't want to end up as a cuckoo's chick for ever, do you?'

'Maybe you're right,' Petrog smiled. 'Maybe I need to get my legs under the table somewhere while I've still got boots on my feet.' The bar was emptying. 'Another bottle!' shouted Petrog across the room.

'I don't want any more,' said Gregor. It was quieter now. Only two or three cigarettes sent grey ribbons curling towards the ceiling.

The bottle came: they drank a glass each. Gregor's head was setting like the sun upon his chest. Even his aches and pains were bearable in the muggy warmth.

'Yes,' mused Petrog. 'I suppose I will just head back home for the time being.' He took a deep breath from the top of his glass. 'It's better to have grass growing all over your paths than not to have any paths at all. But I just don't understand you, Gregor. A nice girl like Alice and you far away from her, cavorting like some giddy goat. I'd go back to her if I were you. Then again, only you know your own mind, Gregor, but as I said... Hey! Gregor, are you listening to me? Wake up!'

'What?' said Gregor looking up with a bemused smile. 'What did you say?'

'Go back to sleep,' said Petrog peevishly. 'I'm off to bed.' He picked up the half-full bottle and his glass and walked towards the bar.

Gregor drew his hand across his forehead and stretched his arms. 'I don't know at all,' he announced yawning.

The door snapped shut behind Petrog. Gregor began to feel that people were looking at him. He started to feel rather exposed but told himself he was imagining the prying eyes. He didn't worry about it for very long, though. The alcohol and the tiredness came to his aid and he was soon slipping slowly down on his side on the bench.

'Put a coat over him, Will,' said the woman who sat on a high stool at the corner of the bar with a cigarette between the tips of her fingers. 'I hope this one isn't a puker.'

The man behind the bar put away his dishcloth and lifted the bridge. He took a coat left hanging on the partition rack and threw it over Gregor who was sighing contentedly to himself on the bench. 'What about his pockets?' asked the man, looking up at the woman.

'Leave him this time,' she advised, tapping a little roll of ash from the end of her cigarette. 'We'll see this one again, I wouldn't be surprised. He's probably in league with that other rascal. I bet you they're up to something.'

'Gypsies, that's what they are,' said the man coldly.

'Oh, you're such a racist,' she spat back. 'You and your gypsies. What the fuck does it matter who they are, Pen Hwch? Have you ever refused to sell anything to anyone?'

'Yes,' said Will Pen Hwch. 'I always refused to sell things to people who can't pay for them.'

'There we are, you see,' she smiled in triumph. 'You are just so stupid. Why did I ever marry you, I wonder?'

'For my money,' said Will Pen Hwch dejectedly.

She tossed her hair over one shoulder and re-crossed her legs. 'Well that's gone now, hasn't it?' She drew another cigarette from a long packet. 'What the hell am I doing in this dump? A girl needs her comforts, you know.'

'Well, I may be stupid but you're just materialistic,' said Will. 'You used to call me "gold of my world" once, but now I'm lucky if you manage the occasional "loose change of my purse"'.

'Oh, shut up, Pen Hwch.' She put down her glass and glared at him. 'If it was not for me this place would have fallen apart years ago. You're fucking useless and you know it.'

'Don't talk so loud,' said Will Pen Hwch going up to the bar. 'Customers might hear.'

'What customers?' she hissed, looking spitefully around the empty bar. 'Go and do something useful and leave me alone.'


Mist was wriggling on the barbed wire. Fog was swirling in the willow branches. These were the only things. Fencing wire, tree branches, stones in the road: these were the only things that punctured the womb of cloud that enveloped him as he walked. White fog was churning and turning like the colours in a soap bubble. From the ditch-side out of the mist, two rushes rubbed their necks together like swans. He sucked the cold moisture into his nose; the sound seemed to fill his head. Even the scraping of his heel on the road was deafening. He could actually hear the joints of his body creaking as he walked. He stood still and listened again. Sounds filled his ears, a stream of pins falling upon a lino-covered floor. Was it in his head or was it coming from the other side of the mist? He could not bring himself to shout out. He simply listened to the static of his being moving through him as the tape of his dreams wound forward.

In the mist he felt that he could reach out and touch the highest tips of the branches on the bank. But when he stretched out his hand he caught nothing but empty coldness. He had not walked very far. Maybe four or five miles? Fifteen? Twenty-five? Had this all happened somewhere before? If only this castle of mist would open its drawbridge and set him free. If only the birds would sing. But birds don't sing in the mist. And crows don't sing at all, like ravens they just caw. Does the nightingale like the cold mist? Perhaps it's because no one hears or sees her that people always praise her voice? Night is probably more romantic than the day. Siôn Eos the Nightingale Harpist was hanged one early misty morning. He was killed under a foreign law. Dic Penderyn too, of course. If they'd died in their beds who would still remember them? Small consolation to them, though. They would have preferred to live and be forgotten. Why don't they teach you your own country's history at school? Instead of boring stories of other people's kings and queens. Can the mist be lifting? Or is it getting thicker? Groping and feeling now, not even the branches visible. What was that smell through the mist? A smell of burning. The world is strange without sound or sight. Petrog might have been right, after all. This was an inhospitable region. Fine for Petrog, of course, on his way home by now: he would land on his feet as usual. People cope in different ways. I am me and I'm here. Maybe it was all a dream last night, but no, or my head wouldn't hurt so bad. I'd take a good drop of the hard stuff right now, that's for sure, to drive a bit of heat into these bones. Damn this ache all down my back. Anyway, I can't really be lost, not when I can smell smoke. Where there's smoke there's a fire underneath it, that's what they say. I'll get something to warm me, maybe even rest a while. Those were sparks. Is it a chimney on fire?

Gregor's thoughts cleared as the mist fell away.

The houses were burning brightly at the far end of the square, red flames licking at the walls. The wild conflagration was reflected in the jagged teeth of broken windows as the smoke snatched at curtains waving farewell. The square shone brightly where the fire had shaved a semi-circle of frost from the smooth cobbles.

The burning was at it fiercest, the tongues of flame leapt from its red throat and no one stood there to restrain it. Only the fire lived in this village of empty shells. The light of the flames played on first-floor partitions revealing past lives within. He wanted no explanation. He did not even want the warmth to heal his aching bones. He wanted to escape. So he turned his back on the dying square and strode back into the mist which closed around him. His steps carried him up through the mist and out above it and he found himself climbing a road that rose gently out of the valley towards distant hills. Below him he saw black smoke billowing from the houses and orange sparks flying. Stars shone out of a clear sky. A fat moon hung over the hills. The mist was slowly retreating back down the valley like a hunch-backed army.

7

**E**ven with curtains drawn the redness of the flames penetrates her kitchen and dances on the china plates on the dresser. The only sound she hears is the hissing of the peat fire on the hearth. She sits at her table, pleating and unpleating her skirt like rosary beads between her fingers. Her turn cannot be long in coming... What's that? A scraping of feet in the farmyard? She raises a corner of one curtain and her heart rises to her throat. She sees a shadow flickering past a whitewashed wall. Through the trees, down in the valley, the village burns with a deep red glow. The branches form a mesh around the fire. Swarms of stars fill the clear sky. She touches the white lace cap on her head. Was that another shadow? The shadow of a man, coming towards her, looking for her? The belt of his coat hangs down limp behind him. A leather bag dangles from his left hand. He walks towards the house, passing through a patch of moonlight, his face looking up at her. His pale face glows like the edge of a knife; he shakes and shivers. Either he is sick or drunk - or mad. The mad ones are the worst, they kill you just for fun. Slowly, very slowly, she lowers the corner of the curtain and picks up the carving knife from the kitchen table. Two knocks ring out. The knock is not hard, but have a care, the wolf's friend is a lazy shepherd - don't let him fool you. She backs up to the dresser, the knife behind her, and calls him in. The door creaks open; he stands shaking on her threshold. His right hand goes into his trouser pocket. Is it a gun, a knife? She will strike first. Her knife flashes up, she runs at him to plunge it in his neck, he steps aside. His hand comes up, he has no weapon, it is just a coin or some shiny bead...She lowers the knife. He backs down one step, holding out to her in the moonlight one silver button. She drops the knife and takes it from him with both her hands.

Here is the dresser with the blue and white plates; the hearth with its peat fire hissing. And here he stands, where he had stood before. His sweaty clothes seemed to violate her clean kitchen. He wondered where the strange feelings he felt came from. There were three of them here then, when the words flew out of the window. She was alone now, it seemed. She made him some tea. It slipped down his throat, warming him. It had a faintly mossy taste, not unpleasant. She was a young girl then, now she was a woman, but her costume remained the same. She wore the same style lace cap, embroidered bodice and heavy pleated skirt falling from a tight waistband. It almost seemed that the clothes had grown with her. He felt his bones thaw out in front of the fire, but the pain in his back seemed there to stay.

'Things have changed, and yet it's the same,' Gregor said. He did not know if Iwerydd had believed his story.

'Don't start telling me about your dreams again, Gregor, I've had enough of dreams,' she said. 'The worst times for me are when I see him again in dreams and we're still happy.'

'But the button proves it,' insisted Gregor. 'I must have been here when it happened. And haven't I described it as it was then? Your father reading from his great book, and you and your mother watching as the words were escaping...'

'My grandfather, it was,' said Iwerydd. 'They were my Nain and Taid, may they rest in peace.'

'So you do remember?'

'I don't know. Sometimes we would be visited - when Taid told his stories - but then they'd be off again. There was a young boy once. He just watched the words coming off the page and walked away without a word. We never saw him again. Perhaps it was you. I get confused. I don't have the memory of the ones without books like Dail Coed. He's the last of the storytellers in the White Land of Hills. That's what we call this place, you know, not the North Country.

'Yes, I know,' said Gregor.

'This was the happiest place in the world at one time,' she continued. 'Before the missionaries condemned our ways and the laws ensnared our lands, before the world breached our walls and drove away the swans that nested on the lake. You know, when they first came to this village one bright Summer morning they lined up the people on the village square and we knew then what would follow. So the village pipers climbed unobserved onto their upturned barrels and began to play a lament for our country, and what did they do to them? Two of their militia went over to where they played and thrust their bayonets through their chests and shoved them into their own barrels. But the bagpipes continued playing to the very end of the song. And they took my Deicws from the fields and cut his head off with a saw they had taken from the saw pit and his blood ran red on the ground. His blood is on their hands and nothing will wipe it off. And that's how it is here, now Gregor.' Her lips were tight and her eyes bulged in her head.

'Didn't you think of leaving with all the others?'

'What the hell else do you think I thought about?' demanded Iwerydd. 'Of course I thought of leaving. But I had to stay. Some people can lose their roots, others are forced to lose them. But not me. So they can just come and get me. I'll not move one inch in their direction. And when they come I'll pay them back for what they've done. I'll claw out their eyes with these ten fingernails and spit in the holes until they cut me down. Maybe it won't bring him back but at least it will avenge him. All I want is one of them, that will do. It was going to be you, until you showed me Deicws's button. The White Land of Hills is not the place to linger across farmyards at night. Perhaps they will never come back, who knows? The worst may be over.'

'I suppose you have to live in hope,' he said, not knowing what to say. He was very tired. Rain pattered lightly against the window.

'You may think I'm weak,' said Iwerydd.

'No, ..'

'I'm like a hard-boiled egg inside.'

'Like an egg?' Gregor struggled to keep his eyes open.

'Like an egg,' she repeated. 'When the cuckoo shoulders

eggs from a nest they smash on the ground but a hard-boiled egg won't break. It will only crack.'

'You must be brave to stay here alone.' He tried to move into a more comfortable position on his chair.

'Staying here does not take bravery,' she said dismissively. 'Only stubbornness.'

'Well, you know what you're doing...' He was too tired to think what to say next. The monotonous beating of the rain on the roof slates lulled him; the quiet hissing of the peat fire coaxed him to follow the twirls of smoke. The Du Traheus had told him man had found language in his dreams. He knew that whales sang to one another, it was the oldest song in the world. Perhaps they found their songs in dreams as well. But where did the singing of the sea in a shell come from? He could almost hear the sea in the sighing of the fire. He was light and free. It was good to swim free. He swims across the room upwards towards the ceiling. Looking down, he sees her sitting patiently. At the table he sees himself, arms folded, head on his arms. He sees the rainwater dripping through the roof. Like smoke from the chimney he flows out into the night. Below him he sees the farmyard and the house and all the dark countryside. The wind raises him; it blows him towards the border. Stars tickle him as they get tangled in his hair. He is at the mouth of the tunnel that crosses under the mountains. The gates are open: he is among a crowd going through. 'Hey, you!' shouts a guard. Someone points at him. He is grabbed by the elbow.

'Gregor, don't fall asleep at the table.' She let go of his elbow.

He started and sat up. A warm feeling was spreading from where she had touched him. 'Sorry,' he said. 'I'd better be on my way.' He struggled to his feet and stooped to pick up his bag. His back was killing him. A droplet fell into a pool of water that had formed in the middle of the floor. 'You've got a hole in your roof,' added Gregor pointing to the water.

'Are you all right?' asked Iwerydd. 'You move as if you were made of wood.' She took no notice of the water at her feet. 'Taid had a story about a wooden puppet...' She looked at him again. 'But come, you must be hungry. What sort of a welcome is this? It didn't used to be like this, Gregor.' She motioned for him to sit back down again. 'People of the road did not need to put a cross on our gateposts in older days.' Rain began to trickle like tea from one of the rafters. 'You'll go nowhere tonight, it's pouring with rain.'

'I'd get that roof fixed if I were you,' said Gregor sitting down stiffly.

She brought bread, butter and pickled cabbage from the back kitchen. 'Mend the roof?' she said. 'That's true. But you can stay the night even if you can't fix it, Gregor.'

'As it happens, I probably could, but...'

'Then that's settled.' She opened the big chest and rummaged in it for blankets. 'You can sleep on the settle and fix the roof in the morning. We used to put travellers in the barn but there's hardly any hay left.'

Occasionally soot would loosen in the chimney and fall softly onto the fire. The rain had eased. Water dripped from the rafters like chippings thrown into a drowned quarry. His thoughts swam across his mind like clouds across the moon. If only the aching in his bones would ease and let him sleep. Black weights weighed down upon his forehead. Just when he had the chance to sleep he couldn't close his eyes.

Eventually the crows began to croak and grey light began to infuse the window and polish the china on the dresser.

'Good-morning,' said Iwerydd, stepping from the darkened chamber behind the partition as if she also had been waiting for the dawn. Her clogs clapped across the slate. She bent to uncover the fire and pulled the cauldron over it. Into this she poured water from a pitcher and threw in a fistful of oats from an earthenware pot. 'We'll have porridge,' she said. 'You'll need something warm inside you while you're on the roof.'

Gregor remembered his promise. He got up painfully and drew his fingers through his hair.

After breakfast, he struggled out to take a look. A few slates had slipped, that was all. He got a ladder in the barn and went to look for tools in the cowshed. The cowshed was warm with animal smells. He made out the shape of a cow. She mooed at him and insisted that he patted her neck. He found a hammer and some nails in a box on the wall. Nosing around outside, he found a second ladder, a roof ladder, in the dank grass behind the house. He would not be long now pushing the slates back into place and hammering new nails into the old holes. But as he placed slate on slate he found he had to take off others higher up until he had stripped a section up to the ridge tiles. Well, he thought, he was only an architect, not a craftsman. Black clouds were gathering above the hills to the North. He scratched his head and tried to work out a system. By the time he had got the pattern established he could smell the rain. Once he knew what he was doing it took only a short while to finish the job. He hammered in the last nail as a raindrop struck his cheek. Once down on the ground, he stood back to admire his work as the rain spattered onto the slates.

'No rain will come through that, Iwerydd,' he announced proudly looking up at the ceiling. When he looked at her he saw she was pointing to the ground where a pool of water was already forming under the window.

'I haven't got to that part yet,' said Gregor, realizing he needed to make a few finishing touches. 'To tell you the truth I'm not used to this sort of work. I haven't the skill in my hands for it... It's not that I don't understand it in theory...'

'I'm sure you can do it all,' said Iwerydd in a calm voice. 'Maybe you'll fix the stairs while you're at it?'

'What stairs?'

She nodded towards the back of the house.

Gregor got up to have a look. He should have noticed there was a loft in the far end. It should have been obvious from the high window in the gable end. 'It only needs a few new steps putting in,' he said. 'I'll fix it for you tomorrow, after I've finished the roof.' He noticed her questioning expression and added hastily, 'If that's what you want, of course.'

The next day when he examined the roof he found, as he'd hoped, that it was simply a crooked slate letting in the rain. He soon repaired it. Being busy with his hands, he found, helped him forget other things.

Having repaired the roof, he went to find tools to measure and cut the stair steps. He spent a while taking the rust off a saw and sharpening it and then went to cut some old boards he'd found in the hay barn. He got them to fit quite well. It was late by the time he'd finished. So what if he was a slow worker? He had plenty of time.

Iwerydd suggested that he climb up the stairs and sleep in the loft that night. The horse-hair mattress was a welcome change from the settle. Eventually he managed to take his eye from the eye of the moon through the window.

He awoke suddenly, not remembering where he was. Sunlight through leaves played on the blue partition. From below came the sound of clogs scraping and the squeaking of a close fitting door. He remembered everything. As he got dressed, he found the pain in his back was even worse for a good night's sleep. He limped downstairs and found himself back in the half-light of the kitchen.

Fingers of sunlight were now pointing at the fireplace and weaving silk stockings in the smoke. Iwerydd got up with a smile as he came in. Her smile was gentle, but her eyes seemed far away. Whenever she laughed he sensed something missing in her voice as though it came from a long way away. He thought of the sound of the sea in a shell.

'No boiled eggs for breakfast, then?' he asked to break the silence.

'It's not a matter to be made light of, Gregor.' In spite of her scolding there was a glint in her eye. 'Now come to the table and eat.'

Gregor watched the light fill the window as he ate his porridge.

'It's going to be a fine morning,' said Iwerydd.

Gregor nodded. 'I'd best be on my way.'

She put her teacup to her lips.

'Is it true you don't like to be photographed?' Gregor asked light-heartedly.

'Whatever will you think of next, Gregor?' she asked. 'What do you think we are, vampires?'

'I just asked,' said Gregor. 'I heard it somewhere and thought it was interesting.'

'Interesting?' She glowered at him. 'That's what the tourists said about us.'

'Well, I'm not a tourist,' said Gregor.

'Do you believe everything you hear?' She turned to the hearth and picked up a pair of shoes that had been drying there. 'Your shoes are dry anyway, without cracking.' She passed them to him. 'I'll walk with you for part of the way.'

On the bank of a pond, Iwerydd stopped under a willow tree that spilled its branches over the water. 'My ducks once swam this pool,' she said, staring into the depths as if she was searching for them there.

Gregor put down his bag.

'The chicks would come stumbling and whistling when they heard the clank of the food bucket. There is little whistling of chicks here now.'

He followed the line of her eyes as she looked up at the tree.

'In these willow branches the thrush used to sing of a Summer evening. Over there on the blackthorns the blackbird would sing back. They won't sing here again, Gregor. Their nests are on the floor and their eggs broken. The hands of men did this to me, Gregor. The same hands that took my gates from off their hinges; the same hands that took my Deicws from the fields. They took the sun out of my sky and the stars out of my night. Why did they leave me here after taking the ground from under my feet?'

Gregor sat on a stone by the pool and looked at the little waves. He couldn't form words around his thoughts. 'I could work hard,' he said eventually. 'I'd be willing to do anything.' He looked up at Iwerydd. 'It looks as if you could do with another pair of hands around here...'

She didn't seem to hear. She seemed emptied of emotion. He followed her back to the house.


He knew there was no shortage of work to be done. If only the aching in his back would ease up. He should probably rest more often but he didn't want to appear as some kind of weakling. She'd probably just think he was being lazy. The work clothes she'd given him didn't fit very well. Baggy, white-pleated trousers that closed tight at the knee, and straw-filled black clogs that made him at least an inch taller. He worked through the days mending and fixing things. He repaired the cowshed roof, put the door back on the barn and re-hung the gates. One day he took a roll of wire and went to patch the boundary fences. Another time he found half-a-dozen emaciated sheep trying to find a way down from the mountain. By the time he had got them back to the Winter pastures it was getting dark. The candle in the kitchen window glowed yellow in the dusk. On the breeze he thought he heard the sound of birds.

He was looking forward to the salted pork, pickled cabbage and potatoes he'd been promised for supper. Their aroma met him as he crossed the threshold. He felt light-headed and a hot wave rushed through him, making him tingle all over. He put his hand to the door partition to steady himself. 'Smells good,' he said. Little red pinheads danced before his eyes.

'Are you all right?' asked Iwerydd, frowning.

'Quite all right,' groaned Gregor through clenched teeth as he keeled over and fell in a heap on the smooth slates.

He was spinning in space. There was nothing but a treacle black night all around him and a lake of treacle ensnaring his feet when he tried to turn. Vague horizons appeared between earth and sky. He began to see stars winking at him above the stain of dawn. A smooth road now wound between hills in the East. Mountain tops floated like islands above the mist. He walked past homesteads but he could not remember their names. The sun's edge peeked at him over the hill crest, whitewashing the slate roofs on the valley side. Little Alice was waiting for him there; she was beckoning him to follow her. The sun was white on the dew and droplets sparkled gold on blades of grass. They were over the hill now, going down. Gregor's shoes could get no purchase on the wet grass. He was slipping and sliding. It was not grass, it was fine sand. He was sliding down through layers and layers of coloured sand like the sand in a glass ornament. He hated to spoil the coloured patterns of the sand, but he had to burrow his arms into the grains to keep himself from slipping over the edge of the precipice that opened beneath him. The valley below was small and far away. He looked over his shoulder and saw the path of his body as it fell through the grains of sand that dropped away far below him into the void. There was nothing to hold on to but sand. That was when he found that he could fly. He could lift himself above the precipice. The farm was down below him to his left. He swooped lower and saw Iwerydd standing on the farmyard shading her eyes against the sun. She raised her hand as he swooped over the rooftops. He tried to call out but no voice came. The sheep in the corner of the field scattered as his shadow passed over them. He noticed with satisfaction that the fences were quite presentable. As he glided through the sky he found his path slowly descending until his feet touched down and he could bend his knees and stand. The sun had retreated and fat-bellied clouds were squeezing the remains of a shower around him. He was by a stone-built village. From where he stood in the road a stile led into the fields. Although he saw no one he sensed there were eyes following him. He realized he was only wearing his big white night-shirt. The wind caught at it and slapped it around his legs. His feet sank into the deep soil of the ploughed field. He saw Alice crossing the field towards him. She called his name. A lump came into his throat as he saw her standing there, her arms and legs pink through her wet white cotton dress. 'So easy,' she said accusingly. She shook a lock of hair from her face.

'Alice, please don't...'

Iwerydd was crossing the dark soil towards them.

'Gregor?' asked Alice.

'Please, Alice, listen...'

'Gregor?' asked Iwerydd.

Gregor turned away from them. Petrog Spalpin was sitting in the shade of the bank, whittling a stick. 'I don't know,' he said. 'But you'll regret it anyway.' Petrog turned towards the two standing in the field. 'This has nothing to do with me, you know.'

The three of them closed in a circle around Gregor as if waiting for an answer. 'Come on,' demanded Petrog, planting his finger in Gregor's ribs. Then Lleucu, the Station Maid, came over carrying a tray. She began to hand out glasses of sweet white wine. 'We haven't got all day,' said Petrog, prodding Gregor again. He turned to the Du Traheus who was standing behind him.

'Didn't I tell you there's no turning back,' said the Du Traheus.

Gregor looked away from them all and saw the clouds swirling slowly up above. Rain drops were spitting on his face and the breeze played in the blackthorn blossom on the hedgerows. He saw the mountains climb like vipers into the dark sky. Alice's voice sang quietly in his head: 'At the tips of the blackthorn trees there are pure white flowers...' the words melted away into the wind. He was rising like the mountains, rising over them through the clouds, far above them towards the place where the light and the dark combine and the spirit walks barefoot through the dew towards the place where the road ends and the paths lead onwards to the stars.

8

From the shaded banks she collects slender leaves of betony. At the field's ends she digs for the roots of wild valerian and the roots of meadowsweet. She shakes the loose soil from them and places them next to the round pennywort leaves and the long roots of goatsbeard in her basket. She knows where to look; it is not long before she collects all she needs. The symptoms suggest a fever. Here are the things to cool the fire in his blood. It must already be deep inside him, probably it has been building a long while. There is a deep confusion in his dreams. The words he speaks through these dreams could be incoherent ramblings or the inner workings of his soul. She knows how to read the hearts of men. She hears other voices talking with his lips. How can she know who they are? She does not recognize the names but imagines the faces. Maybe it matters because she has been so alone. Why did this one have to walk into her world? He might slip out again without so much as goodbye. His life, she knows, is in her hands. She fills both nostrils with the dark smell of soil and roots and leaves that fill her willow basket. These are the herbs to purify the blood and draw out the beads of sweat like marbles on his forehead. Death has ravaged this land long enough. New sparks of life can still be struck on these ancient stones. Her lips move quietly as she pushes open the weather-beaten door.

Gregor's dreams slowed to a violent whirl. He could sense places beyond their emergencies. Memories reclaimed their places from the spiralling white stars. As shadows fell upon him, the stars faded. He blinked twice and opened his eyes. Iwerydd's face was over him. He saw her through the shadows that passed across his thoughts like clouds upon the sea. She placed a cool hand upon his forehead. He felt the clouds parting, his eyes slowing to focus on the walls. When he tried to sit up, her hand on his forehead forbade any movement. When he lay back again she withdrew her hand, lifting a finger to her lips. Rain was splattering the window panes. 'Iwerydd,' said Gregor weakly, 'I'm not well.'

'Don't we know it ?' said Iwerydd. 'Do you think you might try to feed yourself tonight? Hold this spoon.' She got up.

Gregor put his hand to his chin. He recoiled. 'What's this?' There was an urgency in his voice.

She turned at the door. 'Shaving is a very worldly thing.'

'I don't wear a beard!'

'A beard suits you,' she said.

'Have you got a mirror?'

'You don't trust me?'


He fed himself with a spoon that evening but it was a few days before he got up.

The day Gregor put his work-clothes back on it was pouring with rain.

'A good time to get better,' was Iwerydd's only comment as she stared out at the rain. 'If it's fine tomorrow you'll be back in bed again!'

'So you want me to go out into the rain just to get wet? At least the rain doesn't come in any more.'

'Come Gregor, are you really so serious as you look?' She pulled up a chair for him. Its feet scraped across the slates. 'Bess is milked, the water drawn and we have peat enough for today.'

'Sorry,' said Gregor. 'It's just I know I have been more trouble to you than help. There was I thinking I could be of help to you.'

'Was that what you thought?'

'I didn't want to burden you, Iwerydd. It was just easy to be here, that's all.'

'I'm glad you're better, Gregor.' Iwerydd put his porridge on the table in front of him. 'I'm just sorry you couldn't have been a bit quieter about it, that's all.'

'Quieter?'

'All that noise in your sleep.' Iwerydd put some porridge into another bowl. 'You had not mentioned Alice to me before.'

'Hadn't I?' Gregor looked out at the rain. 'Did I say anything else?'

'Is Petrog your brother?'

'I haven't got a brother. Just a friend.'

'Why were you saying "Please, don't" all the time?' Iwerydd turned towards him. He was still looking out of the window. 'You have such a silly voice when you plead.'

'I don't know, Iwerydd.' Gregor turned to look her in the eye. 'All I remember is seeing stars turning and turning and going out one by one. Then I was here waking up in bed and your hand cooling my forehead.'

'Only you know your own thoughts,' she said. 'I'm not even asking you to share them. I don't need to know them to know you.'

Gregor wanted some time to think about it all. He was not well enough to work. By afternoon the showers had cleared and he said he needed to cut the grass each side of the path. His clogs rattled across the farmyard. A vicious wind was poking him in both sides. He didn't even try to work but sat by the pond and watched the ripples move to the shore. He knew he had been ill. He was weak; he had to drag his feet along. Even the stone he sat on hurt him and the sky was cold. He gave up and struggled back to the house.

'Are you all right?' asked Iwerydd, emerging from the back kitchen as he clambered up the stairs to his room.

'I'm fetching something,' he said. He didn't want her to

hear that he was breathless. He only needed five minutes rest. He sank back into the mattress.

An hour later he was still there. Half an hour after that he felt a lot better, but needed something to do. He reached down, felt around and drew his leather bag out from under the bed. Like a lucky dip he plunged his hand into it and fished around. He propped himself up on the bed. 'Iwerydd,' he called. 'Where is it?'

Clogs tapped upon the stairs; in a moment she was at the door. 'What's the matter?'

'My things?'

'Things?' She turned up her nose with feigned disgust. 'Is that what you call them. Dirty washing is what I call horrible things like that.' She put a finger and thumb to her nose. 'Oh, and there was some box in there with knobs on it.'

'Yes,' said Gregor. 'My radio.'

'Was that important?' asked Iwerydd.

'Yes. Where is it ?.

'Radio, was it ?' said Iwerydd breezily. 'A worldly thing like that.' She turned to go. 'I chucked it...'

'Oh you didn't, Iwerydd' broke in Gregor angrily. 'I needed it. You probably don't even know what a radio is, do you?'

'I do very well,' said Iwerydd calmly, 'what else did those tourists have when they used to come around recording our folk songs? And if you might just let me finish the occasional sentence, I was going to say that I'd chucked it into the drawer underneath your things there.'

Gregor pulled open the drawer. From beneath his underwear he extracted the radio-set.

'Are you happy now?' asked Iwerydd.

'Yes,' said Gregor. 'But why is my radio wrong if your singing is okay? Isn't singing also quite a worldly thing?'

'If that were the smallest of our sins we'd be a good people,' she retorted as her clogs clipped down stairs.

When she was safely downstairs he switched it on and turned the dial. All he got was the breakfast sounds of frying bacon and eggs on every wavelength. 'Damn it all,' he declared, holding his ear close. Only once did the very tail-end of a voice reach him through the static. Maybe it would work better in the open air.

When he got downstairs Iwerydd was quite horrified. 'What would Taid say?' she demanded. 'Worldly things have no place within this home.'

'Give me a break,' said Gregor clutching his radio protectively. 'Why do you invoke your Taid every time you want to put me down? And anyway, I'm sure you're not all the angel you make out.'

'I don't believe in angels anyway.' Her annoyance was not concealed. She pointed to the door. 'Go out, will you, to play with your stupid toy.'


The radio channel he'd found spoke in another language from his own. He knew the words but they said little to him. There was the occasional jingle-jangle and some Radio Sgingomz sung out all the time. A droplet of rain fell on his nose from the eaves. Another fell on the black face of the radio. Gregor used his shirt sleeve to wipe it off. In his hurry he had forgotten his jacket. He could not stay outside all evening, she was angry rather than hurt. He might as well try it inside, downstairs. The best place might be by the kitchen window above the valley.

He ventured inside. She took no notice. The best place turned out to be on the third shelf of the dresser opposite the window. Iwerydd did not interfere although she made no pretence to be listening. He listened to the words in all the familiar languages. There was music. He only needed a second to recognize two guitars struck fine and light. He held the band and listened to the song. She was standing, listening.

The words were full of regret and longing. It spoke of travelling alone through Winter in the North.

Gregor held out his hand to her. 'Why don't we dance to this song?' he asked.

She stepped out of her clogs and took his fingers in her hand.

He kicked off his own clogs and sank an inch towards her.

'Dancing is not "worldly"?' said Gregor.

'You know how to dance?' she asked.

He nodded.

The tips of her fingers were light against the back of his hand. The touch of her skin felt good. He stepped towards her and then away as the song swelled and flew around them. He could feel the words around him as he looked at her and heard the singer say the sun was in her smile and all the moon was in her eyes and he couldn't help but believe it. Barefoot, they moved gracefully hand in hand across the floor. The song told him to look for the sun in her smile and to watch her eyes to see the full moon rising. Between the bars of song, the whistle of a curlew came from the mountain. It was a mournful sound. She held him close. Her skin through his shirt was soft. The song asked him to look again for the sun in her smile and to see again if the moon had risen in her eyes. The song melted into the background, surrounding them in its warm glow. Perhaps it was being alone that was bringing them together. The moment between them had no beginning or end. There was no pause in their barefoot dance. No signal foretold the coming together of their lips.

She remained in his arms long after the song had finished.

'I've always liked that song,' said Gregor. They let go of each other's hands and stepped apart. He turned towards the window where he saw his reflection in the panes of glass.

'I suppose you danced to that one with Alice?' Iwerydd spoke in a matter-of-fact tone.

He drew his fingertips across the cold glass. 'And Deicws?' he asked quietly. 'Didn't you dance with Deicws?'

'Yes,' said Iwerydd. 'Sometimes I still dance with him in my heart.'

'I've danced to that song with Alice,' said Gregor. 'And

anyhow, I'm sure you don't have any room in your heart to dance with anybody else.'

'There just might be a little room left,' said Iwerydd.

'How much?' Gregor held his finger and thumb a centimetre apart. 'That much?'

'Don't play games, Gregor,' she scolded. A new tune began to play. 'That's our mountain tune,' she said with a shudder. 'Come, we must dance to it.' She held out her hand.

Her bare feet glided like a curtain in a breeze across the slates; Gregor did his best to follow her movements. He realized that he was not a very good dancer. He barely managed to move his feet in unison with her intricate steps. He was glad they weren't on some dance floor. People would have noticed his clumsiness. The last note lingered in his ears.

'You dance very well,' she said.

'I don't suppose you've got anything to drink here?' he remarked as they sat down.

'Plenty of cold water.'

'Nothing stronger?'

'You mean alcohol?' She looked at him in surprise. 'What a suggestion! A worldly thing like that.'

Gregor was a bit flustered and almost failed to notice her smile. She laughed out loud. 'You're an easy one to tease,' she said, touching his cheek. 'There's some tonic wine Taid used to swear by in the dresser if you want it.'

She brought out a bottle, half-ful, and handed it to him. He got two cups down from the shelf.

'Not for me,' said Iwerydd. 'I don't need tonic wine. I'm not ill.'

Gregor sniffed the wine. 'You will be after drinking this,' he smiled. 'Go on, have a drop.'

They finished the half-bottle. It was not too bad, just a bit sweet for Gregor's liking. He got up to look for some more. There were several full bottles; he took one. He needed a drink to calm the fluttering he felt inside him as he sat next to her at the table, occasionally touching her hand.

In her room later Gregor fumbled with the buttons on his trousers, his back to Iwerydd who was already under the sheets.

'You don't need to be so shy,' she said.

Gregor got out of his clothes and jumped into bed. Her skin on his skin was like cream on strawberries, her warmth comforted him like a Summer day. They found each other's lips. Their tongues caressed; they breathed the same breath. He kissed her cheeks, her neck, her shoulders; he kissed her breasts, her arms, her stomach. He kissed her until her heat burnt his cheeks. She writhed as he played his tongue over her satin skin. As he drew the tips of his fingers down her back she curled taut as a bow. Their hearts which had trembled like a captured thrush now churned and dived like a Ferris wheel. 'You're so warm,' she said, stroking his face. 'You're so warm, Gregor.' There was a dance within them as their bodies met. They melted together like a ball, as round as the world and as warm as a nest. They were hot as the sun and head over heels, so near and still too far in their white passionate love.

They woke up together and looked at each other. His clothes were still on the floor, her lace cap lay on the stool. 'I've got a headache,' she complained, rubbing her head.

'You're just not used to it,' said Gregor, looking at the empty bottle next to her cap on the stool. 'It was quite a find, that wine, wasn't it?'

'Tonic,' she corrected. 'Taid never drank wine.'

'I think I love you,' said Gregor.

'You think you do?' she said in feigned surprise. 'How much?' She put her finger and thumb half an inch apart. 'That much?'

'Don't mock me,' said Gregor smiling. 'I know I love you.'

'You don't know me.' She reached down for something to put on.

'I've always known you,' said Gregor. 'But it's even better now I've met you.' He drew his hand down her arm. 'Have you ever seen the sea?'

'Of course I have. And I've been to the city.'

'With Deicws?'

'We weren't supposed to go. Luckily no one saw us.'

'No one?'

'No, or the story would have got back. You don't see many of us in the city. Well, you didn't in those days at any rate. Our people are probably thronging the place by now, searching for a new world. And I'm still here. What difference does it make, Gregor? What does it matter where we happen to be if we arrive together?' She put on her blouse and began buttoning it up. 'The best rising is an early rising,' she said. Gregor watched her smooth white legs move towards the door. She turned back to look at him. She was too far away for him to reach out and touch her. 'Come back, will you?' he pleaded. She took a few paces back towards him until she was within a few feet of him. He stretched out his arm and his hand brushed her knee. She took another step forwards. He slid his hand between her knees and stroked her leg, drawing her closer still. She sat almost on top of him and drew her fingers through his hair and over his forehead and his lips and over the stubble on his chin. He held her to him. She was soft and warm through her thin blouse. Without speaking they lay in each other's arms. Gregor stroked her skin under her blouse. His thumb filled her armpit and then his palm moved over her skin, softly down her side, across her belly, over her hips and all along her legs. When they kissed her tongue was hot against the inside of his mouth and over his teeth. He breathed in as she breathed out. They were two rivers in the dance of their confluence. Two seagulls riding the same tide. They fitted perfectly together like a box; a knot tied with expert hands. A two part jigsaw of quicksilver. Their hearts churned like a water-wheel with sunlight bursting over it and turning all its foam to jewels.

For a long time afterwards neither of them moved until he finally turned over on his side.

At the kitchen table, the closeness that had been between

them was edged with uncertainty. Everyday things like putting lumps of peat on the fire or drawing water from the well seemed different, and this feeling accentuated their unease, frightening them. Their careful politeness with one another was strange. They had not evolved their own lover's words with which to address each other. They both started speaking at the same time. She laughed.

'What?' he said.

'No, you say,' she insisted.

He held out his hand to her. 'Why don't we go for a walk?'

She looked at him. 'Where to?'

'Just for a walk, it doesn't matter where to.'

'What?' Her eyes widened. 'Walking for no purpose? Like going around and around the farmyard?'

'No, silly girl.' Gregor laughed. 'You know what going for a walk means. It means going for a walk. Come on, it's fine outside.' He got up.

They walked down towards the valley, holding hands. Once over the brow of the hill, they saw the tops of the trees rising out of the ravine. The purring of the full river came through the trees. The trees were like fishermen bent over the water. A large bird slipped from a fencing stake in the wall. Its wings were heavy until it found the wind. A buzzard, not a kite, he decided. He stood watching it as it attained the high world of its own. She had walked on ahead. When he looked back, he saw her white cap bobbing up and down from behind a wall before disappearing around a corner. There were no sheep or cattle in the fields. To the West the sky was yellow through bars of cloud. He stumbled after her down towards the ravine where the boom of the river met him and filled his head. Under the branches it was like a tunnel. 'Iwerydd!' he called, but the swollen river swallowed his voice. He smelt damp leaves. Perhaps she was waiting for him around the next corner; she would leap out at him, laughing...

'Winter is long, days are short,' he thought, as the bones of trees appeared out of the shadowy banks. The path descended almost to river level, winding around boulders and black pools. Going down on his knees on the banks, he drew his hands through the silken water, cupping it in his hands and burying his face in its coldness. Shaking his head, refreshed, he hears dogs barking above the noise of the river and he smells peat smoke on the pungent river air.

The barking stops. He hears a slapping of water more high pitched than the dull rolling roar. The vague form of a woman appears at the riverside with a white shirt in her hands and a deep stain on the shirt. No matter how hard she scrubs, the stain remains. Presently she rises to her feet and looks in his direction.

'Iwerydd?' he asks.

The washer woman points her finger towards curls of smoke which drift grey against the blackness of the trees. Two droplets of water form at the end of her finger and fall back into the pool.

The smoke seemed to be coming from a large building he now saw above the riverbank. As he approached he saw there was light in the back window. It was some kind of mill, but the huge water-wheel was still. When he turned there was no trace of the girl by the pool.

He knocked a couple of times at the mill-house door.

It opened and Iwerydd stood on the threshold. 'We've been waiting for you a long time,' she said.

'Why didn't you wait for me earlier?' asked Gregor. 'What are you doing here?'

'Going for a walk with you,' she said. 'So I called in to see Dail Coed. What's the point of going for a walk unless you call on someone on the way?'

'Welcome, Gregor,' said a stooped old man who he presumed was Dail Coed. 'Come in and have some tea.'

'Thank you, Dail Coed,' said Gregor looking around. There was a nice fire blazing on the hearth.

'And don't address me in the second person plural, Gregor,' said Dail Coed. 'There is only one of me.' He sat down in the corner of the fireplace. 'It's not our way to use the polite form around here.'

'Sorry,' said Gregor pulling up a chair.

'I expect you're here on behalf of the Du Traheus.' said Dail Coed presently.

Gregor sat up in his chair. 'Well, yes, I guess so,' he said. He wondered how he knew about that. 'To tell you the truth, I'm not altogether sure what I'm doing here...'

'Thanks, Gregor,' said Iwerydd.

'What I mean is,' he hastened, 'I'm not entirely sure what I'm supposed to be doing on behalf of the Du Traheus here. I had to leave in a bit of a hurry and somehow or other my detailed instructions failed to materialize...'

'Detailed instructions?' laughed Dail Coed. 'From the Du Traheus?' He leaned over and got a bottle out of a cubby-hole in the wall. 'The Du Traheus couldn't direct you to the nearest bus-stop, Gregor. The only thing he's good at is knocking back plum brandy.' Dail Coed set three glasses on a wooden tray. 'I don't suppose you're one for the bottle at all, Gregor?'

'Yes, he is,' said Iwerydd. 'He's quite shameless. And shame on you too, Dail Coed, for encouraging him.'

'A mill is a sociable place,' said Dail Coed. 'This was the best place for a pint of cask brew in the district.' Dail Coed handed round the glasses. 'Farmer's sons need more than oatcakes and buttermilk to make them strong.'

'You kept a tavern as well, then?' asked Gregor.

'A pub!' Dail Coed spat into the fire. 'What an idea! A worldly thing like that? I did not sell drink.'

'I'll bet you didn't give it away,' said Iwerydd.

'In Gofannon's name, what's wrong with giving things away?' demanded Dail Coed. He topped up Gregor's glass. 'People were kind in those days. I would give them beer and wine and brandy and they would give me wheat and barley and corn. I lived well.'

Gregor swallowed half his glassful. 'This apple brandy of yours is pretty good stuff,' he said. 'Tell me, Dail Coed, am I right in thinking you're also a good storyteller.'

'I am not just good at anything,' said Dail Coed putting down his glass. 'I'm an expert. I am the best miller, the best storyteller and the best wine-maker, beer brewer and brandy distiller in the country.'

'I see there's no law against boasting, anyway,' said Gregor quietly.

'Modesty is one of my virtues!' shouted Dail Coed. 'Boasting is a deadly sin.'

'You won't get the better of him, Gregor,' advised Iwerydd. She turned towards the old man. 'Are we going to get a tale out of you tonight, Dail Coed? Won't you tell that one you used to tell when I was a little girl: that one about the hounds by the river ford?'

Dail Coed composed himself in his seat. 'A long time ago,' he began, 'shortly after the island had been divided, Urien Rheged went to the woods to hunt. And the name of the place where his hounds came to drink was the Ford of the Place of Barking. And in older times all the dogs of the countryside used to come to the banks of that ford to bark, and no one dared to look at what was there until the King came with his hounds to hunt. And when he came to the banks of the ford he saw nothing but a girl washing the blood from the shirt of the one she loved so well. And the more she washed the shirt, the darker the stain became. And then the hounds ceased barking, and Urien seized the woman and had his will of her; and then she said, "A blessing on the feet which brought thee here." "Why?" said he. "Because I have been fated to wash here until the stain be gone. And I am daughter to the King of Annwfn, and come thou here at the end of the year and then thou shalt receive thy child." And so he came and he received there a boy and a girl: that is, Owain, son of Urien and Morfudd, daughter of Urien...'

'Excuse me...' said Gregor, interrupting him.

'Don't interrupt!' said Iwerydd.

'Yes,' said Dail Coed and he told that tale word for word exactly as it had been. They spent the night partly in laughter, partly in seriousness, and all their drinks were old and all their food was fresh and the last morsel was as sweet as the first morsel. 'Let me not live,' said Dail Coed as the dawn broke through the trees, 'if there is a single word of lies in any of it at all.' He pressed a rounded stone into Gregor's hand. 'Give this to the one that seeks it from thee.'

A wind from the high pastures blew down on them as they emerged from the trees and climbed the rugged path between stone walls. It was probably the same easterly wind that had cleared the sky of clouds. An ancient horse hung its head over a wall, watching them, its eyes rolling. It was no more than skin and bone. Gregor turned away from it in fright. A pink glow was growing above the hills. In the West a pale crescent moon was surrounded by three stars.

9

The grey sun is sinking through the mist. A green swelling breaks through the mist like a boil under the skin. On the top of the mound the Du Traheus sits cross-legged. The trees' fingers reach out towards him and the hissing and howling and roaring and neighing of animals surrounds him. Gofannon the Wright, the divine craftsman, approaches him offering spirits and bright wines from golden goblets. If only he will show him the stone. 'I will not show it,' says the Du Traheus. And Mabon fab Modron, the Great Son, approaches from the wall of mist dragging his chains behind him and asking the Du Traheus to let him touch the stone against his fetters and set him free. 'No,' replies the Du Traheus. And then Lleu Llaw Gyffes, the Bright One of the Skillful Hand, places between them a chessboard and chessmen and they play for the stone. The Du Traheus, as lord of the animals, calls his own chessmen from the woods and the bushes but Lleu, Lord of light, reaches out his wide hand to confuse the circle of the sun and the stars, and in the snare of time the Du Traheus is caught and all his flocks and herds are subjugated. The stone falls into the bright hand of Lleu. The lightning returns to his finger tips. 'Yes,' said the Du Traheus. 'For now the adder stone is thine.'

As the days lengthened they would often wander the hills and woods. Iwerydd tried to teach him the names of the herbs and the flowers and to explain their uses. And only sometimes would the past overtake him as he watched her. His lips would tremble and he would turn away. At other times they would call on Dail Coed and listen to his tales. Gregor sensed that she could read the words that played on his lips. It helped Gregor to forget all his dreams. At first light he would listen to the dawn chorus and sense the great earth slowly turning towards the Spring.

Gregor only went down to the village once. It had been raining softly all morning. He followed the cart track back down the way he had come. Green weeds marbled the black cobbles of the square. No crows cawed. The stink of damp soot hung between the bones of the houses. At the end of the square there was a building taller than the rest from which a tower rose like a finger pointing to the sky. Looking around, he soon located the iron hoops where the pipers' barrels had been. They were red from rust and black from fire. He didn't stay long.

When he returned he said nothing about the village. He felt a strange sense of loss every time he thought about what might have been. The transience betrayed him. He kept thinking how sad it was that nothing he valued was going to last. The happiness he felt when he was with Iwerydd was always overhung with the shadow of their inevitable parting. Their paths had crossed but each was eventually heading in different directions. He had to tell Iwerydd what he felt while he still knew what he wanted to say. Picking up the bucket of water, he hurried across the farmyard. 'I don't want to lose you, Iwerydd.' was all he could say when he got inside.

'Your hand is cold,' she said, taking the bucket from him. 'I'm glad you came, Gregor. But I've always known you were going to leave. I wouldn't change the things we've done, but it's made me weak. I know what you're going to say. I've known all along that you had to go. So go now while Springtime covers up our gravestones. I'll not stand in your way.'

Gregor took both her hands in his. 'Will you come with me?' he asked.

'When it's all over will you come back with me?' she asked.

It was early May. The trees were powdered with tiny leaves. The air smelt dry and warm. As they crossed the farmyard, the unfamiliar rumbling of machines could be heard coming from the village. Blue smoke was rising above the trees. They walked in the opposite direction, towards the purring of the river.

'So you've come to say goodbye?' said Dail Coed as they sat down. He reached for a bottle in the hole in the wall.

'Did Gregor tell you?' asked Iwerydd.

'Some things don't need telling.' Dail Coed poured out a measure for each of them. 'But Gregor is right that you should leave. There is nothing left here. Soon they'll be back to wipe out the few that are left.'

'We heard engines coming from the village,' said Gregor.

'Let's drink to your future, then,' said Dail Coed.

They struck glasses.

'It's your turn to propose a toast, now,' said Dail Coed.

'Long Live the Old Order!' said Gregor raising his glass.

'The Du Traheus taught you that one and no mistake,' said Dail Coed, laughing. 'He's still looking for a path back through the brambles, poor fellow.'

'He was very good to me, anyway,' said Gregor. 'I wish there was something I could do for him.'

'Your chance may come,' said Dail Coed. 'Have you still got that stone I gave you?'

'I doubt I'll ever see him again,' said Gregor. 'We're heading North to the Capital States.'

'According to Gregor that's the land of milk and honey,' explained Iwerydd.

'You'll never make it,' said Dail Coed emphatically.

'Why not ?' demanded Gregor.

'Have another drink,' said Dail Coed. 'You won't get close to the Capital States, friends. What about the desert they've created between us and the border? What about the soldiers and their foreign laws? You're not tourists travelling in air-conditioned coaches with escorts and itineraries. There are no northbound crossings any more.'

'I've got skills,' said Gregor. 'I'm not afraid of hard work. Don't they welcome people who are willing to work?'

'Their welcome is to kill people,' said Dail Coed.

Iwerydd took Gregor's hand. 'Well, wherever we go, we'll be there together, won't we, Gregor?'

'It would be a shameful thing for you to take Iwerydd to a place like that. You should go down to the City like the rest of them, get a crossing to the New World. There's no future for you in the North. And give my regards to the Du Traheus.'

'If we see him,' said Gregor.

'What about you, Dail Coed?' asked Iwerydd.

'They will come for me, I suppose,' he said. He drank from his glass. 'But they won't find me. You can't catch shadows.'

'Will you look after Bess till we're back, Dail Coed?' asked Iwerydd.

'I'll milk her and feed her and look after her like one of my own. Come tomorrow, about the time the dusk is falling. We'll take the buggy downstream over the bridge. I'll get you to Tafarn-y-Bwlch in a couple of hours. You know your way from there, Gregor?'


The blue bells shook their heads as they watched them walk away along the path by the pool. Gregor carried most of the bags, Iwerydd was still wondering if she'd explained everything about Bess to Dail Coed. The sheep and lambs would be fine - the gate to the mountain was open for them. Iwerydd insisted on putting down a cold fire ready to be lit when they got back. It was their way, she explained, whenever they set off on a journey.

Gregor had to leave his radio-set on the dresser so that he too had something to return to. She locked the door.

Dail Coed was already sitting bolt upright in the driver's seat waiting for them. The old horse pulled wearily at bunches of grass it found growing out of a stone wall. Its ribs were clearly visible through the stretched skin. But once they got going it proved less fragile than it looked and hardly slowed down even on the steepest hills. Once they had climbed from the ravine, a clear night opened about them and the high pastures spread before them under a cold moon. As they bid their farewells outside Tafarn-y-Bwlch, Gregor noticed the moonlight glinting in Iwerydd's eyes and realized she had tears in her eyes as she kissed the old man goodbye.

The bar was big and gloomy. It was also empty. Gregor pushed their packs onto a bench. The landlady sat on her high stool by the corner of the bar. A cigarette lay next to her in an ashtray sending up smoke in a thin spiral. She looked Iwerydd up and down, then turned to Gregor. 'You didn't come back empty handed, I see,' she said. She turned away and picked up her cigarette.

Iwerydd glared at her.

Gregor took a step forward. 'Have you got a room available, please?'

'We've got lots of rooms available,' she replied, putting down her cigarette again. 'Do you want it by the hour or is it for the night?'

'How dare you!' said Iwerydd, her face pale as snow. She turned to Gregor. 'What sort of a dump is this, Gregor? I'm not staying here.'

'Go back to the North Country then,' said the lady. 'See if you can find somewhere better. We've had better types than you here, Miss, and I'll bet they charged higher rates.' She sipped her drink, calmly.

'Shut your foul mouth,' said Gregor loudly.

'Hey!' The landlord came in from the back with a mop in hand. 'What did you say, arsehole? Get the hell out of here. We're closed.'

'Piss off, Pen Hwch,' said the lady to her husband. 'I'm dealing with this.' She turned back to Gregor and Iwerydd. 'So it was a room for the night you wanted, then? That one who said he was your partner only used to book rooms by the hour, so I assumed...'

'I'm not staying in this pit,' said Iwerydd.

'Look, I'm sorry if I got you wrong. That friend of yours said you knew all about it...'

'Petrog Spalpin?'

'Could be.' She lit another cigarette. 'Yes, I think he used that name sometimes.'

'We were never partners,' said Gregor.

'Well he left you his bill, anyway,' she said, fishing out an envelope from a ledger on the counter. 'He said you'd be back to settle up.'

Gregor took the envelope and opened it. 'The bastard,' he said.

'And you made out this was a good place to stay,' hissed Iwerydd in Gregor's ear.

'This must be your quiet season,' said Gregor as he tried to work out what to do about the bill.

'Nobody comes this way any more,' said the lady. 'We'll be busy again when the peace-keeping forces come back, though. The "disturbances" won't close us down.'

'Look,' said Gregor, 'I can't pay all this.'

'That's pretty obvious,' said the lady. 'Give me half and you can pay up front for your room tonight as well.'

'You have no right to charge me for his...'

'Listen, nobody has any rights any more. Do you want to stay or what?'

'This is outrageous,' said Gregor.

'Just for the one night, is it?'

'We need a lift to the station tomorrow morning.'

'Maybe Sionyn Troliau will take you,' she replied, leafing through a dark ledger on the counter in front of her. 'Sign here,' she said.

The next morning they woke early. It was grey outside. Iwerydd complained of pains in her stomach.

'Probably something you ate,' said Gregor.

'I didn't eat anything, did I?' She half-turned away from him.

She was probably annoyed at Gregor for wasting all that money on someone else's account. Or perhaps it was just that time of the month.

'I've missed a month,' she said.

'Oh, ' said Gregor. He sat on the edge of her bed. 'How?'

'You didn't seem to need lessons.'

'But we were careful...'

'You don't have to worry,' Iwerydd cut across him. 'You don't have to stay with us.' She turned and seared him with her smouldering eyes. 'You're free to go any time if we're such a burden to you.'

'You're not a burden,' said Gregor. He was trying to fathom his own feelings.

In the tavern yard they stood while Sionyn got his cart ready for the downward journey. The mist swirled around them, its white sheet tearing on the rocks. 'On a fine day you might be able to see the sea from here,' said Gregor, indicating the direction with his hand. 'If they ever had a fine day.'

She sat on their bags, pleating her skirt between forefinger and thumb. 'Put your arms around me,' she said. 'I'm so cold.'

'Will we make the early train?' asked Gregor.

Sionyn Troliau looked at him and then turned away to spit. 'What train?' he asked. 'There are no trains.'

'How do we get to the city then?'

Sionyn Troliau raised his whip and slashed the pony on its rump. She neighed angrily and shook her tail.

'Don't whip her!' said Iwerydd.

Sionyn Troliau said nothing.

'Why aren't there any trains?' demanded Gregor.

Sionyn Troliau shrugged his shoulders and stared into the mist.

'It's like talking to a stone,' said Gregor in disgust.

'Want to walk then, do you?' said Sionyn Troliau. 'Or do you want to pay me extra to take you to the distribution point at Croes-y-Mynydd?'

'Why there?'

'Lorries stop on their way to the coast.'

'They'll pick us up?'

'If you're lucky.'

'How much extra?'

'That'll depend,' said Sionyn Troliau, rubbing his chin. 'The more questions you ask me the higher the price will go. I don't like people asking me things, okay?'

'I noticed,' said Gregor. 'Just take us there.' The fine rain was cold on the up-draught. He put his arm back around Iwerydd's shoulders. They listened in silence to the hollow sound of the pony's hooves and the grinding of the wheels.


The distribution point at Croes-y-Mynydd turned out to be a shelter badly built out of breeze-blocks, seemingly left unfinished. Half-a-dozen thin men lounged around taking no notice of the rain. Gregor saw that concrete posts or pillars had been placed across the road; the men sometimes carried more from a pile by the building. One of the men recognized Iwerydd and came over. 'Hello, Hywel Draws.' said Iwerydd.

'So you're leaving, Iwerydd? Are you with him?'

Iwerydd nodded. Gregor held out his hand. Hywel Draws looked at it.

He explained that the lorries were due. The peace-keepers were heading out of the Northern sector. The fighting was officially over in that area. What difference were the blue helmets going to make anyway? The fighting had only just begun. They could at least give him and his men a lift down to the coast. Hywel Draws nodded towards the concrete obstacles across the road and smiled. His men prowled around, making no effort to conceal their guns. He explained that going by lorry would take about fifteen hours on the mountain back-roads. The main road bridges had been blown up months before.

From the upper reaches of the valley the rumble of trucks became audible through the rain. From the hanging mist a line of crawling lorries descended like ants crossing a log. Each time they reappeared they were bigger. The men stood on the road in a line in front of their concrete pillars. The first pale-blue lorry roared around the bend so fast Gregor could feel its heat. The men stood jeering side by side in the road, arms outstretched or fists striking chests. The lorry's horn blasted out long and loud. The air-brakes shuddered. Hands behind the screen waved them to one side. The men on the road were engaged in a mad game of chicken with one other or with fate. Not one moved. They grimaced and shouted at the charging machine. They held their fists high in the air. The lorry was upon them now, sending chippings flying in all directions, tyres screaming. The men dived backwards, rolling clear. The cab slewed away, plunging the side of the lorry into the concrete pile.

As the first lorry hissed, the second pulled to a stop behind. Automatic weapons appeared at the windows. The megaphone crackled on; a voice commanded the men to clear the road immediately or face grave consequences. The men slapped their thighs and laughed. Hywel Draws walked up to the cab. He showed them his open hands and smiled.

The tarpaulin kept some of the rain out but not the night. Somewhere high on the mountain Iwerydd shared out the blankets she had brought. The men passed around their country brandy. The lorry lurched and bumped; everyone kept getting thrown together in a heap. The brandy was rough, but warm inside. Gregor passed the bottle back to one of the men. Even when the road was smooth, the rain swished down around them and found its way past the tarpaulin to their skin. At least it was free.

Soon after dawn Gregor poked out his head. It was no longer raining; the clouds were all in the West. Flat land lay in all directions. The houses were divided by gardens, not by fields. They were entering the suburbs. When a pale sun came up the windows that remained gleamed dully. Many of the houses were burnt out; charred rafters pointed like fingers to the heavy sky. The convoy rolled on; there was no one out on these early streets, no cars, no trams. The streetlights were unlit. Only in town did Gregor see pedestrians on the pavements. They pretended not to look up to watch the lorries pass. Their skin was grey, as if they were covered with a film of dust.

He slid back down to Iwerydd's side. The men in the back of the open lorry kneaded the caps in their hands and chewed tobacco. They did not flinch when an explosion rocked the air.

Gregor stuck his head out to see what had happened. Smoke was pouring from windows half way up one of the apartment blocks. Iwerydd was tugging at his sleeve.

'We're nearly there,' she said. She was collecting their things together. He did a final check on their documents. His address book was in Iwerydd's bag. With her papers and his card in his pockets plus some hard currency, he would soon get them a ticket out.

Hywel Draws ordered a couple of his men to roll back the tarpaulin. Above them the remains of an apartment hung over the street. An iron bedstead was held hanging by one leg, the bedclothes like Rapunzel's hair almost touching the ground. Gregor was surprised to see lights in café windows in the midst of all this mess. Shops were opening; even a woman on a street corner selling flowers. At the foot of some steps by what had been a fountain some boys kicked a ball and shouted, pointing to a makeshift goal.

'I was here only once before,' said Iwerydd. 'It seemed full of light then.'

'You walked towards me hand in hand,' said Gregor. 'Your smile filled my eyes.'

'No more dreams just now,' said Iwerydd. 'We've got a boat to catch.'

The man closest to her leant over. 'Got tickets then, have you?' he demanded.

'No, but we'll get them,' said Gregor.

'You've got papers and money then?' The man thrust out his hand. 'Come on, show us what you've got.'

'Leave them alone,' snapped Hywel Draws. 'We're fighters not thieves.'

'Why are you leaving then?' asked Iwerydd.

'Look, my pretty. We'll be back in the hills soon,' said Hywel Draws. 'You can't fight without proper weapons.'

'You sound so brave,' said Iwerydd. 'And where were you when they burned our village?'

'What could we do against the militia? But if they want to keep the White Land of Hills they will have to pay a high price for it. You can't kill a shadow.' He raised his fist above his head. 'Better death than shame!' he shouted.

The others raised their fists and shouted the same slogan.


'No,' said the booking clerk. He pushed the form back towards Gregor. 'Read my lips. It's not been stamped. Go away.'

'Is there some problem?' enquired Iwerydd, moving closer.

'Yes,' said Gregor. He showed her the unstamped form. 'He says I need my supervisor to validate it for foreign travel.'

'Give him ten dollars,' said Iwerydd. She pushed her face into the ticket kiosk. 'What bullshit is this?' she demanded, pushing Gregor's ten dollar bill into the tray. Her white lace cap was reflected bobbing in the glass. 'Just issue the tickets, okay?'

'Yes, ma'am,' said the clerk. 'Something can be arranged.' He pushed the ten-dollar bill into his breast-pocket and pressed some buttons.

Out over the harbour the sky seemed to be melting into the sea. The Sea Swallow's ties strained against the quay. Pre-embarkation was already a long wide queue. It was strange to be back in the middle of a crowd. Here and there the white caps of the women bobbed up and down like water lilies. In his city clothes Gregor felt conspicuous in the midst of all the native dress. He almost regretted leaving his borrowed clothes behind. Touts forced their way through the crowds selling snacks, tickets and drinks at all kinds of prices. Someone jostled him until he tripped over some packs and someone sprawled among them. He apologized and rejoined the queue. The line was moving up towards the booth by the gangway. These people didn't require dogs and guns to send them up the steps. Some of them had no luggage. Gregor imagined them standing watching their lives burn inside their houses. The blue helmets didn't stand in anybody's way. He looked towards the six pale-blue lorries parked against the wall. Tour of duty over, going home. Out to sea, pewter-coloured waves bounced in the harbour; a grey horizon fell into the clouds. When they got to the booth at the entrance to the gangway Gregor put their bags down and presented their travel documents. They were waved on upwards towards the ship. Gregor gave the documents to Iwerydd and ushered her forward as he manhandled the baggage back around his shoulders and into his arms. There were people behind who were becoming irritable and impatient with his fumblings. 'Get a move on,' somebody said gruffly. 'Leave the bags, we'll carry them,' said someone else. The crowd laughed. He struggled after her to the top of the stairway onto a gangway on the side of the ship. The crowd below milled around, encampments were established, some had cooking stoves. On the gangway, a single-file queue moved towards a revolving gate with iron jaws. The gate took one person at a time so Iwerydd passed Gregor his documents and stepped in. The gate made a metallic click as it turned and locked. Gregor pushed their bags into the next compartment. When the gate turned again he followed. The gate closed around him.

'Ticket. Papers,' demanded a busy voice from behind the wire.

Gregor slapped his ticket and library card on the shelf.

There was a bit of movement behind the wire as someone seemed to be examining things one at a time. A window opened and two eyes stared at Gregor. The window slammed shut. Gregor's documents were back in the tray. 'You need a stamp,' said the voice. 'Access denied.'

Gregor tried furiously to explain. He even tore ten dollars out of his pocket and stuck it in the tray. He pulled out all the notes he had and tried to push them in. They were rejected. The sickening metallic click squeezed him out into the daylight like a pip from a monkey's mouth. He grabbed at the bars and shook them wildly, but to no avail. People were pushing him away. Looking down he saw the white faces of the crowd turned towards him, like sunflowers towards the sun.

He found someone in uniform at the bottom of the steps.

'You need to get a stamp,' said the man in uniform. 'It's not that far, the library. You've got plenty of time.'


Gregor ran through the city. Craters scarred the streets. Occasionally he heard what sounded like gunfire. There was black smoke filtering up above the eastern quarter.

At the library the gates were locked. 'Du Traheus!' he shouted, kicking the bars with an angry foot.

'What is it?' came a sleepy voice from the little window half-way down the steps.

'Open up!'

'You on the register?' yawned the voice. 'Put your library card on the sill.'

'I work for the Du Traheus. Open the gate.'

'Why?' asked the sleepy voice.

Gregor made a quick upward movement of his chin and rolled his eyes. He shoved his hand into his pocket. 'That's why.'

The heavy oak doors to the Mythology Department creaked apart. A light hung over the Du Traheus as he bent over a low table with a bottle in his hand; he was pouring something black into two liqueur glasses. 'Ah, now,' he said looking up. 'You know, Gregor, this is actually the best vintage, although not the rarest. Tell me what you think.' He handed him a glass.

'Very nice,' said Gregor, slugging back the contents of his glass. 'Listen, I need a stamp. Please hurry. I don't want to lose her.'

The Du Traheus took the form that Gregor held out for him. 'Of course I'll help you, dear boy.' He sipped his drink. 'By the way, how did it go in the North Country?'

'I haven't got time for that,' said Gregor between gritted teeth. 'Can I have that stamp now please?'

The Du Traheus poured out another glassful for each of them. 'You didn't get killed, then?'

'It went fine,' said Gregor.

'Did you bring fables?'

'Another time, okay?' Gregor tried to get the paper back from the Du Traheus. 'I need a stamp.' He prodded the paper with his finger. 'Right here, Du Traheus.'

'What other time have you in mind, Gregor?' asked the Du Traheus. He climbed up the pulpit steps and pulled out another bottle. 'I'm afraid it has to be exactly at this time, if you don't mind. You're still employed here, remember. Present your report or leave here relieved of all your privileges and expenses.'

'What expenses?' said Gregor.

'How was Dail Coed?'

'Fine, fine...' Gregor realised there was no way past this one. 'He sends his regards.'

'Yes.' The scholar tapped a hard nail on the table. 'And what else besides?'

'Quite a lot, actually,' said Gregor, suddenly feeling tired. 'Lots of stories. I can't remember all of them right now. He told us about the washerwoman by the ford.'

'At night, yes,' said the Du Traheus, 'Go on.'

Gregor did what he could to convey the main themes of Dail Coed's stories. As he remembered them he saw again the words like songbirds rising from the page as if they were flying out of a rusty cage. He heard the curlew cry from the dark mountain. In his pocket his fingers closed on the smooth stone he got from Dail Coed. 'He said it was all true. And he said: "give this to the one who seeks it from you." I guess that's you, is it Du Traheus?'

'Very good,' said the Du Traheus. 'What took you so long?' He took the stone gracefully in his hairy paw. From his pocket he drew a brown paper envelope. 'Your expenses,' he said presenting it to Gregor.

Gregor took the envelope. 'Du Traheus, can I have that stamp now?'

'Pulpit, top drawer, left,' said the Du Traheus. 'Be so kind as to bring it to me.'

Gregor ran up and tore the stamp from the drawer. He jumped down to the Du Traheus and held the paper in front of him. 'Do it,' he shouted.

The Du Traheus took some soot from a box and rubbed it on his forehead. He moistened it with saliva, took the stamp and plunged it into the mess. He brought the stamp down on the empty circle.

'Will that work?' asked Gregor in disbelief.

'Get back to the ship,' said the Du Traheus. 'Why didn't you give me the stone straightaway? You knew I couldn't ask outright for it. If you'd have given me it earlier we could have talked some more about other things.'


Gregor scrambled up the steps into the street and raced along wide moonlit streets. He was chasing an ebbing tide. He saw the ship straining at her moorings, he would leap the stairs and run towards her and push his fingers through her hair and see her smile. He flew over the rubble and the rubbish filling the streets. He raced down towards the harbour. Eventually he turned the final corner and stood still. He stared at the long path of moonlight that stretched from the empty harbour to the white ocean.

10

The houses are so happy to be rebuilt, so ready to slip back under the gentle whitewash. The houses don't like the dust that settles in the corners and blunts the sun's glint on evening windows. It was better before the dust. It was better when it rained even though everything got soaked. Wet or not, we stood our ground, not like the mothers and children huddled together on the square and the fathers separated to one side with their hands on the napes of their necks. Yes, we heard the shooting. Were we not shot at ourselves? Did we not have our insides ripped out by fire? Still we stood, even though we were empty. This was not our first twist of fate. Forever coming and going: that is the thing with people; restless things compared with us the houses. We will remember them, though, we'll remember the ones that built us. But who remembered about us? Rain came in; no one came to mend the roof. Who cared that the jackdaw made his nest in the chimney and sent twigs spewing out across the floor? While our timbers cracked and our walls bulged no one cared any more than the brambles and the flowers. Soon all you'll see will be our stones like gravestones down the valley, sinking slowly back into the earth from whence we came. Even then we will not forget; our memory is in the stone and our skin knows the touch of the red hands that first raised us and pushed us slowly into place. It was neither earthquake nor flood that despoiled us but fountain pens between long fingers. Disembowelling us with explosives was work for an afternoon. The decay that followed was uneventful. Until today when echoes are heard of the time that we were built. The scrape of stone on stone awakens us *from deep slumber. Foreign voices are scraping against a blue sky. Clouds of dust rise. Engineers, builders, carpenters. Men in yellow hats peering at grey papers. Ask as you do this: have you the right? Your forefathers did not build us. It is not your memory which our stone contains even though your aspirations are all along our valleys. Come, if you will, come rebuild us; put us back here stone by stone. Without us you are as chaff upon the wind. Graft your new vines onto old roots. Possess us. You can write your own history books now, no one will know. But hurry now to clear this debris that shows the imprint of the heel you turned in our soil. Repair the houses, plant flowers on the river banks. Put new fish in the old pond. Say nothing to your children. We will not forget. Our memory is in our stone; the touch of the red hands that raised us is on our skin. Your soft fingers will not erase it. The houses are so happy to be rebuilt, so ready to slip back under gentle whitewash. Do you think that you are the ones that will rebuild us?*

Gregor stood on the quayside watching the boat that had brought him turn away. Seagulls screamed overhead. He did not wave, he shrugged. He was back home and his hands were empty, without even a bag. He would have to face up to telling Alice that things had changed. It would be difficult. He did not look forward to it. He could not have stayed in the city. The library was closed, and for all he knew Ostán Laban might also be shut down. He hadn't checked, he'd got the next boat out. A boat back home had been easier than finding a ship to follow her. At least here he had connections. He would find another ship. He touched the Du Traheus's envelope in his pocket. The library expenses were not bad. And he did now have a ticket to the New World with a valid visa stamped by his boss. Once he had sorted out his personal business he would check out the local shipping lines to arrange a passage.

He scanned the promenade. The Aircol, as usual, was the focus of the streetscape. Sand blew across the pavement. He wandered about aimlessly playing for time, but eventually he had to climb the hill of white-washed houses like steps going up along the cliff-side. Only a few called after him from across the street. Someone raised a hand from a passing car. He was concentrating on what to tell Alice. 'Come clean,' he was saying to himself. 'Open your mouth and blurt it out.' He remembered how Iwerydd used to tell him to learn the words before starting to sing.

White spring sunlight reflected from the laurel leaves; rhododendron buds were tipped with red. He walked gingerly over the crunching white gravel of the drive. The red roof-tiles came into view, followed by geometric slates. He climbed the porch. Inside he could hear laughing voices. A rustle in the garden made him turn. A blackbird was drawing an earthworm from the soil. He rang the bell.

The laughter inside ceased. Footsteps approached.

'Gregor!' Alice seemed pale.

He crossed into the darkened hall.

'We'll go into the front parlour,' she said. 'We've got visitors in the kitchen.'

It was rare for her to invite him into the parlour. The room was colder than in the hall.

'How are you, Alice?'

'As you see me, Gregor,' said Alice without humour in her voice. 'How about you?' She looked him in the face. 'You've been away a long time.'

'Yes, I know.'

'Have you no bags?'

'They are in left luggage. I didn't get a chance to change, I just rushed up here...'

'I'm glad to see you,' said Alice. 'If you want to change, there are some things you left here last time. Go and wash and change.

It bought him a few more minutes. Being clean made him feel stronger. 'I've got to tell you something,' he said when he got back downstairs.

'I see.' Her voice was calm.

'I'm sorry, Alice...It's just I...'

131

'It's just what?' Alice's voice was rising. 'Just having an affair? Is that what is it, just?' She turned from him to stare out of the window.

'I'm sorry, Alice, I didn't...'

She spun round, her eyes glaring. 'Shut up!' She pointed a finger at him. 'And you didn't even have the decency to write. I've learnt a lot about you, Gregor, since you've been gone.'

'I did write, Alice.'

'Oh, I see.' She twisted her lower lip downwards. 'Another one lost in the post, is it? Do you hate me that much?'

'No.'

'It took me weeks to find where you were staying.' She blew her nose into a handkerchief.

'In the city?'

'Ostan something. You must have had a laugh reading my letters to her.'

'I didn't get any letters, Alice. I didn't do any of this to hurt you.'

'Well, that is what you have done, Gregor.'

Gregor bowed his head. 'I came straight here to tell you.'

'That was very noble of you,' said Alice sarcastically. 'Well, you needn't have bothered because I already knew. I knew you wouldn't be faithful.'

'I'm sorry, Alice, you know how I...'

'Know?' Alice cut across him. 'I know nothing about you. You're not the person I knew. You don't care about the desolation you leave behind you. As long as you can fill your own hive with honey. You're not the person I used to love.'

'Please don't, Alice,' pleaded Gregor. 'Please let me...'

'You're a low-down dog, a dog from hell.' Her invective was cut by a knock at the parlour door.

Gregor looked up. 'Petrog!' he exclaimed.

'I see you two know each other,' sniffed Alice.

'Yes, of course,' said Gregor. 'We know each other. How did you find me, Petrog? Someone in town told you I was back?'

'I was in the kitchen,' said Petrog.

'Gregor's been telling me about his new sweetheart,' said Alice.

'Iwerydd!' Gregor looked startled. 'He's not interested in that.'

'Oh, Petrog is very interested in that,' said Alice. 'Why not tell him how interested you are, Petrog?' Alice folded her arms.

'Not that much,' said Petrog reluctantly.

Gregor stared at him. 'What?' he said.

Gregor turned to Alice.

'What's going on?'

'Petrog has been very good to me while you've been chasing skirts.'

'So that's what you meant by "feet under the table",' said Gregor glaring at Petrog who was looking away. 'I should have known you wouldn't pick up the tab, you always leave debts unpaid.'

'I'll buy you a pint,' said Petrog.

'You owe me more than a pint, friend,' said Gregor. 'For the time being I'll ask you only for one thing.'

'What?'

'I want to talk with Alice. Alone.'

'Go to the kitchen, Petrog,' said Alice. 'I can always call you.'


'You've changed,' said Gregor.

'So have you.'

'I'm sorry to disturb your love-nest.'

'Gregor, he was the only one who would tell me the truth about you. You've got a bloody cheek coming here acting like you're the victim.'

'Call your lap-dog back in then,' snapped Gregor. 'I'm off.'

'The truth hurts, does it?' Alice clutched his sleeve. 'Listen, you rat,' she hissed. 'Petrog's told me all about your cavorting with the waitresses at some railway hotel. You threw away everything for a station maid. Did you tell her you don't even have dignity ? Did you?'

'No,' said Gregor. 'Actually I didn't. To Petrog words are currency and he sells them at a price.' Gregor made a move to go. 'So, I'll see you then, Iwerydd.'

'I doubt it,' she said. 'It happened; it is no more.' She held open the door.

'Like a shooting star,' said Gregor.

They almost smiled.


Dusk was falling as he trudged back down towards the harbour. The boat on which Gregor had crossed had long since sailed. He'd heard it was continuing down the coast rather than returning to the city on the other side. The inquiry desk was still open.

'Sea Swallow. Is she on your list, Jack?'

'Afraid not, Gregor.' The clerk looked up from all his schedules. 'Try Pigeon Lines? They operate from the city. We only have current information on Spalpin's Boats nowadays. The rest is unreliable.'

'Spalpin?'

'There's only one Spalpin,' said the Clerk proudly. He explained that Spalpin had made it big over the other side. But he was back and in the boat business. And fair play to him. He hadn't forgotten who his mates were. There were jobs for the boys all round. Things were picking up in town. Pity Gregor had missed out. Still, he might be more lucky this time. Gregor asked what he meant. The Clerk mentioned a local partnership. They had a job up for grabs and some said it was already earmarked for Gregor. What? Gregor didn't even know about it? The Clerk told him to cut the bullshit. Why else was Gregor back in town? Everyone knew he was here for the interview.'

'I'll see you, Jack.' Gregor turned away from the window. He had decided what to do. It was too late now; he'd have to stay the night and head back in the morning. He'd already decided where to stay. It could only be the Aircol. The Du Traheus's expenses would cover it and more. Why not go out in style? He could tell Iwerydd he hadn't crept out of his own country like a whipped dog.

Gregor felt calm as he stood on the Aircol's sweep of marble steps. The Gothic detailing on the facade was interesting rather than beautiful. In fact, he didn't think it was beautiful at all. There were voluptuous mermaids and many kinds of eels and fish tails. He wasn't used to walking into the Aircol through the main entrance. The revolving doors brushed forwards at the touch of his hand and he then stood under the chandeliers in that familiar hall. He made straight for the check-in desk.

'How much for a room?' he asked. The 'Late Availability Rates' on their signboard had suggested they were not full.

'One hundred dollars, sir,' she replied. Her name badge said her name was Alaw.

'Don't sir me, Alaw,' he said. 'My name is Gregor. One hundred dollars did you say?'

'Yes,' she confirmed. 'But we do also have some late availability rates I can offer you.'

'I noticed,' said Gregor.

'Twenty five per cent off chance bookings.'

'You're saying the room costs seventy five dollars?' Gregor looked over towards the bar area. It was more or less empty.

'Are you by yourself?' asked Alaw.

'Why do you ask?' said Gregor. He was trying to catch sight of anyone he knew.

'Because if you want single occupancy you get another ten per cent off.'

'Why?' said Gregor. He was losing interest. The Du Traheus's expenses were one thing but he had already been ripped off once by the Aircol and it wasn't going to happen again. He turned to go.

'Just a second,' said Alaw, showing him another brochure. 'We have a special Thursday night offer available. If you dine here tonight just fill in this voucher and your room will be included in the price of your meal. It's a new concept in hospitality.'

'I'll take it,' said Gregor. 'I guess this new concept must be keeping you really busy?'

She printed out a registration form for him to sign.

He could see his face shining yellow in the brass sides of the elevator. He did not look as rough as he had thought. A shave, some soap and water, that would fix it.

He poured a prodigal bath that overflowed when he lowered his bottom into it. He'd used up the bubble bath and bath salts. The bathroom was like a snowdrift. He used the froth to soap his face and scraped his razor across his face. With the towel around his hips he rummaged through the mini-bar.

He found some whisky miniatures. He wanted it on the rocks so he picked up the phone. In his left hand he fiddled with the television remote control.

'Room service,' said a young female voice.

'This is 407. Can you send me some ice...and I need a tie.'

'Some ice, sir,' she repeated. 'And a tie, sir?'

'Yes, you know, the type you put around your neck. Anything with blue in it will do.' He put down the phone and hit the teletext index button.

There was a hushed air in the dining room, like an audience waiting for the curtain to rise. People were whispering over apéritifs. Gregor knew all about it. He found a stool at the bar.

'You're still here, Steffan,' he said as the bar-tender turned towards him.

'Gregor! What the hell are you doing here?'

'I'll have a glass of champagne, Steff,' said Gregor. 'Have something yourself. Put it on my room.'

'Well, well,' said Steffan, shaking his head.

Gregor noticed that Zwingli was eyeing them up from the other side of the room. Steffan served the drink and busied himself at the other side of the bar for a while.

'Who got my job?' asked Gregor when Steffan returned to his end of the bar.

'Guess, Gregor.'

'They didn't give it to Coesau Hirion? Is he here tonight? I'll soon see what he knows about wine.'

'He only lasted three weeks,' said Steffan. He cleared Gregor's empty glass and discreetly re-filled it beneath the bar. 'They say things about you,' he said, placing the glass on the bar. 'But they don't say you don't know your wine.' Steffan ducked down to get something out of the fridge.

Gregor turned around. Zwingli presented him with the menu and a wine list. He betrayed no recognition of Gregor. 'Are you eating yourself tonight, sir?' Zwingli asked coldly.

'I thought I'd have something from the menu,' said Gregor.

'Sir is most witty,' said Zwingli unsmilingly.

Gregor checked the labels of the wines he had chosen. The vintages were correct. He sniffed his glass. 'It's fine,' he said declining to taste the wine. His bottle of red wine was open on the table.

The Cloudy Bay Sauvignon became even wider and more complex with his smoked salmon. He thought of Iwerydd, wishing her closer. He drank another glass of Cloudy Bay. They took his plate.

The sommelier appeared, coughing politely, and adjusted the position of the red wine in its silver holder.

'Would you like me to pour the red wine now, sir?' said the sommelier. He poured a deft drop into Gregor's glass which Gregor sniffed. He sniffed again and tasted some. It was supposed to be a closed, muscular wine, but this was ridiculous. It smelt and tasted of cat's piss. He raised his head from his glass and noticed that Zwingli was crossing over towards them. The Sommelier stood by waiting for Gregor to nod.

'Everything is fine?' said Zwingli.

'Actually, no,' said Gregor. 'I'm afraid not.' He wiped his lips with his napkin, leaving a purple stain on it.

'Are you actually suggesting that something is wrong?' asked Zwingli in a scoffing tone. He stepped back and stood with his arms folded.

Gregor picked up the bottle of red wine. 'This is not Calon Ségur 1982!'

'Yes it is,' said Zwingli snatching the bottle from Gregor's hands and turning it to read the label.

'It's cat's piss!' said Gregor in a loud voice.

Zwingli almost jumped. 'This is the vintage of the century, monsieur!' he exclaimed. 'This is Cru Classé wine. This is not cat's piss!' When Zwingli calmed down he looked around. It took him a moment to notice the trickle of red wine that had run from the bottle all down the front of his crystal white shirt.

Zwingli looked up again and sent a withering look around the dining room that caused a dozen faces to turn like wilting flowers back to their plates. Zwingli strode back into the service area clutching the bottle. Eventually a complimentary replacement was sent out with an apology. It tasted fine, even better for being free. The lamb was sweet and tender. The mashed potatoes were silky smooth on his tongue. When the meal was over he went to have his coffee in the bar. Sitting there was a familiar silhouette.

'Did someone tell you I was here?'.

'I was watching you in the dining room,' said Petrog. 'Liked your style.'

'Shut up, Petrog,' said Gregor. 'So is this where you hang out now?'

'What will you have?' asked Petrog beckoning to Steffan to come over.

'Something very expensive if it's your round,' said Gregor. He turned to Steffan. 'I'll have a 1966 Baron de Sigognac Armagnac.'

'Make that two,' said Petrog.

'What do you know about boats?' asked Gregor.

'Only that they pay.'

'You've never known how to pay Petrog.'

'You look as if you need a ticket. 'I can get you a ticket any time you like. Free of charge. Gratis. First Class.'

Gregor tasted his drink. It was good. The bar was getting empty. People were taking leave of one another. He said nothing.

'Where do you want to go?' asked Petrog.

'To the city,' said Gregor. 'And that's all I'll tell you. I remember discussing personal matters with you once before.'

Petrog put a card on the bar. 'I'll be seeing you around,' he said. 'In the mean time use this. This will get you over to the city on one of my boats. Any time you like.'

'This thing is probably useless,' retorted Gregor, ignoring Petrog's outstretched hand.


'Anytime you like' turned out to be eight o'clock the following evening. First Class was a bench. Gregor took a long time getting to sleep and a short time sleeping. It was silence that woke him. The boat rose and fell on the waves. The engines were cut. A night light was caged to the wall. Everything was monochrome. He sat up on his bench and rubbed his neck. Boots could he heard clanging on steel. The door flew open before a cold blast of salt wind. The Captain's coat glistened yellow. 'Get up,' he called. 'We're there.'


Once on deck, Gregor saw what he meant by "there". He could see nothing but banks of clouds rolling over a close horizon. Greenish white pinheads of phosphorescence danced in the water.

'This is as close as we can get,' said the Captain. He jutted out his chin. 'The harbour is mined. We're to take good care of you. We don't want to hit a mine, do we? That would not be being careful, would it?'

'Petrog told you, did he?'

'Oh, yes,' said the Captain. 'You're certainly a VIP. You even get your own personal rowing boat.'

Gregor noticed two men preparing one of the boats. 'I can't row that,' he exclaimed.

'It's not far to shore,' said the Captain. He pointed a finger towards a breach in the pillars of cloud. The boatmen stood ready. 'Dafydd Chwith here and Huw Cychod will row you across,' he said. 'We can't use engines in this area.'

Gregor looked at the widening gap in the clouds. There were rocks and trees visible on the shore. The boat fell heavily into the water, pushing a dance of phosphorescence across the waves.

*ar below her she watches the cars draw up at the lights. The crowded pavement is now free to spill across the street. People the size of ants scurry across the city in never ending streams. She turns back to tend the flowerpots on her windowsill. A faint, sweet breath rises from the emerald leaves. Even in this artificial environment her herbs grow thick and fast under her skilful fingers. She bends over the cot to adjust a blanket and smiles at the two glistening, round eyes that follow her every movement. She lifts the baby up and holds her close. She's getting quite heavy; her first birthday isn't that far away. The baby gurgles and points to a toy on the floor. Iwerydd can't understand what is delaying him. She is not that hard to find. He must have got her sailing details from the shipping line. She goes over the same questions that worry her night by night. What if something had happened? What if he'd changed his mind? What if... She has tried every way to trace his movements and has found there is no way. So she waits. She knows that he will come. She puts the baby back down. She will at least be able to show him that she hasn't failed in this new country. Gregor was right; there are opportunities here. He will be proud of her. It is not so hard to see the things they need. Needs that are not satisfied by department stores. Deeper needs that reveal themselves to her in tiny movements of the eye and hand and in certain things they say or leave unsaid. Her hands hold the healing arts she learned from her grandmother. She has in her fingers the secrets of cooling and soothing the mind and body with herbs and flowers, roots and understanding. It was from her grandfather that she learnt the art of listening. And if they are happy to pay for her traditions and are comforted by the touch of her hand upon their hot foreheads, who is she to refuse their patronage? The things she took for granted back home, power of rejuvenation held in fragrant leaves, she finds earn her a living of sorts in the wasting toxic world of the metropolis. Understanding their needs, understanding their fears is her profession and she does it well. Her clients do not see the fragile heart she tends beneath her breast. Sometimes when she thinks too hard she has to close her eyes. Her only cure is to pick up the baby girl and hold her tight. Nearly one year and still no word. Sometimes she can hardly breathe when she thinks of the world she has left behind. She cannot bear to look at her old clothes. She no longer wears a white lace cap. Her life is to cure others now. No one needs to know that her own heart is crushed and small like a ball of waste paper. The telephone rings. She touches the receiver once and picks it up with a trembling hand. The drawling accent wakes her up and she replies in a cheery voice. She jots down a few details, asks some questions and makes a note of all her client's answers on her pad.*

Gregor walked the shore for a long time. Brown smoke climbed up into a leaden sky. As he rounded a headland, the city was suddenly spread out before him. There were fires in several locations. He heard the thud of rockets being fired from the hills above the city.

When Gregor reached the offices of the Pigeon shipping line at the harbour, there was only one man left on duty. Gregor found him hiding in a back office. With the aid of a modest bribe Gregor persuaded the man to accompany him to check out the timetables and shipping lists. The man identified ships called Gwaneg Fôr, Gwanwyn Gweilgi, Mam Doue, Môr Farch, Eryr Môr, Morwyn y Don and Prydwen but there was no reference at all to Môr Wennol.

The clerk removed his spectacles and straightened his back. 'No such name registered, I'm afraid.'


Gregor left the harbour and walked slowly into town. He was wrapped up in his thoughts and unaware of his surroundings until he noticed the mossy smell of the river and heard its rippling. As he looked around he caught a glimpse of light on water through green leaves. He must have been walking aimlessly for hours. He was leaning on the railings that circled the park by the pavement cafés. The world seemed huge and he felt small and cold. Heavy drops of rain fell on him from the twigs above his head. He remembered the nightingale's song dripping down on him that night and then he remembered imagining its beak parting the falling rain. He was glad it was not yet night. He was going to have to find the Du Traheus.

The Department of Mythology was in darkness. Only an emergency light outside the door was still lit. He would complain to someone about the doorman they had in charge of the main entrance. A total waste of another ten dollars, he thought. Ten dollars to get the gates open and then no one inside. Why didn't they just put up their prices on a board and call it a tourist attraction? They probably would once the fighting was over. 'What a place,' he said as he struck a match. He got a candle out of the Du Traheus's pulpit and set it up on the desk. There was a musty smell to the room; Gregor had always felt it was a mistake to build a library underground. 'Du Traheus,' he called out, softly at first and then louder. 'Du Traheus!' He grabbed the candle and went down the aisle to check the area by his old desk. Soft, hot wax fell onto his wrists.

When he got outside it was already dark. 'Where the hell is everybody?' he demanded, rapping at the doorkeeper's window. 'Give me back my ten dollars.'

'I told you we were closed,' said the doorkeeper. 'Anyway, I need the money.'

'Why don't you just charge an admission fee?' said Gregor coldly.

'Look,' said the doorkeeper. 'If you find someone responsible for this place just ask them when I get paid, will you?' The shutter slammed shut.

Gregor walked from the library in the direction of Ostán Laban. He figured he knew the people there and he had enough money to cover the accommodation. He had nothing to hide, and especially as he no longer worked for the library he could do as he pleased. Adam was no longer his boss. The café over the road was dark in spite of a crooked 'OPEN' in the window. He tried the door but it was locked. Crossing the street, he tried the door at Ostán Laban. This time the latch yielded and the door squealed open. A single bulb burned in the lobby. It was very still and quiet. White notepaper lay in piles on the floor and all the way down the staircase. He took up a handful and brought them under the light. 'Why don't you answer my letters?' he read. 'Why don't you send a word ?' He recognized the note paper, and the rounded words of her hand. The letters were strewn all over. He was collecting them in his arms when a peal of wailing laughter rang out deep within the house. It was followed by a sharp scream. Gregor dropped the papers and grabbed hold of the banister as a dark flailing shape hurtled towards him and he saw the white flash of a steel blade. 'You killed him, you killed him, you killed him,' screamed the shape in a frenzied voice.

Gregor vaulted the banister as a meat-cleaver came down biting deep into the handrail where his arm had been. 'Mrs Laban, Mrs Laban,' cried Gregor. 'It's only me, Gregor!'

'Gregor?' Her voice was suspicious. She peered at him from behind long, matted hair that obscured most of her face. 'I thought you were that murderous Sebedeus come to pay his debt in blood. He killed him. I'm sure of it now. If only I could have seen his poor body. We wanted to give little Adam a good funeral. We can't even visit his grave when we've nothing of him to bury. Nobody will tell us anything. Do you know if he's still alive? He might be. How can I be sure about anything? I make his dinner every day. What if he turned up and there was no food for him? You know how angry he gets when he's hungry. He likes his food, Gregor, but he won't wear a bib any more, he's such a naughty boy. But he's a good boy really. He's mama's boy.' She tugged at the meat-cleaver until she got it out of the banister. Gregor noticed there were many hack marks in the wood, as if someone had been chopping at it. She beckoned Gregor to follow her upstairs. 'Come,' she said. 'He's waiting for us.'

Gregor shuddered as her fingernails clawed the back of his hand. She seemed many years older. He followed her upstairs, through long dark corridors with creaking floorboards and across empty rooms. A window opened down over the stairwell. He recognised the door to his old room several floors below. The door was slowly closing.

She pulled him on through more passages and unfurnished chambers. In some, behind the doors, they climbed narrow staircases. At the end of a long passage they came to a door under which he saw flickering light.

A bright fire was burning in the grate. Logs hissed and snapped. Llygad Bwyd sat on a leather sofa. He wore a velvet jacket and a yellow waistcoat. Mrs Laban went over to him and straightened his pink bow tie. She stroked his greasy white hair.

'Good evening, Gregor,' said Llygad Bwyd. Gregor noticed he'd put on a lot of weight. He probably had eaten Adam Laban's suppers when Adam failed to turn up night after night.

'That's enough, now, Llygad Bwyd,' said Mrs Laban. She looked pityingly at the old man and then turned to Gregor, 'He's gone funny in the head,' she said, tapping a finger to her forehead.

'No, you've got it wrong again, dear,' said Llygad Bwyd. 'It's you who's gone potty, not me. Please try to remember that.'

'My husband is as mad as a hatter,' confided Mrs Laban in a whisper. 'The silly coot doesn't realize that himself, do you, dearest?' She tickled him under the chin.

'Stop that, you imbecile,' shouted Llygad Bwyd, shaking his head to ward her off.

'I do apologise for him,' said Mrs Laban.

'I'm very sorry to hear about your son,' said Gregor

'What about him?' demanded Llygad Bwyd angrily. 'Don't listen to her gibberish. I keep telling her Adam's probably just joined the militia and gone up country to kill bandits. Maybe he'll even catch the Du Traheus himself,' said Llygad Bwyd.

'He will come back. He will, I know it,' piped up Mrs Laban excitedly. 'He's never missed a Sunday lunch in all his life, Gregor. He'll come tomorrow. I know he will. We're having a roast rat, his favourite food.'

'Completely batty, I'm afraid,' said Llygad Bwyd with a sigh. 'However, she does cook an excellent roast rat,' he added. 'You should stay for lunch with us tomorrow. She always makes lunch for three. Adam won't turn up. At any rate, I hope he doesn't or I'll be back out on the streets.'

'The Du Traheus escaped, then?' asked Gregor.

'Well, they didn't exactly let him go.' Llygad Bwyd spat into the fire. 'I suppose you're looking for him?'

'Yes.'

'See that door?' Llygad Bwyd pointed to a small door in the corner of the room. 'He's down there.'

When he opened it a waft of cold air billowed into the room. Stone steps spiralled downwards.

'What have you done to him?' exclaimed Gregor, turning back to face the room.

Llygad Bwyd stretched himself, yawned and got up stiffly. 'Come, I'll show you,' he said.

'Why should I trust you?'

'Who said you should?'

Llygad Bwyd went first. Gregor was surprised how agile he was despite his widened girth.

'You were never friendly towards me before,' said Gregor. 'Why help me now?'

'Look, I'm an angry old man at heart,' said Llygad Bwyd over his shoulder. 'I don't have a friendly nature. But that doesn't mean I can't help people. Anyway, what happened to Adam Laban, I'm sure you and the Du Traheus had something to do with it. So I guess I owe you one. He was the reason for my misfortune. Can you believe it ? My own stepson was the reason I had to sleep out on the streets. You did me a favour, Gregor.'

'I had nothing to do with it. Last time I saw Adam he was down there guarding the lobby. Don't go accusing me of anything.'

'Have it your own way,' said the ex-tramp. 'I'm afraid I'll have to leave you here. Just follow the steps down and then follow the path to the very end. Don't turn back.' With a lightness of foot that seemed incompatible with his bulk Llygad Bwyd sped back up the steps, almost as if an elastic rope had been tied around his waist.

'I suppose I'm going to have to take his word for it,'

muttered Gregor. He followed the stairs down and down, his hand feeling the wall all the way. When he got to the bottom he felt the rub of sand under his shoe. He lit his stump of candle and noticed there were no footprints in the grains of sand that seemed to have been blown across the stone floor. The low tunnel was cut through the living rock, jagged edges sticking out from walls and ceiling. When the tunnel became lower and narrower he continued on all fours. Eventually he had to crawl. The roof of the tunnel pressed down on his back, snagging his jacket. The candle was spluttering unhappily in his outstretched hand. When it went out, red spots danced before his eyes. All he could do was drag himself forwards using feet and hands. When he tried to go back he found that the rock's grain was against him and it was like trying to get out of a lobster pot. The walls were pressing in on him. He struggled to fill his lungs. He did not remember passing out. He knew he was very cold. His face was pressed to the gritty floor; his fingers reached out in front of him. Did he hear the trickle of water? Was that a light breeze playing over his fingertips? He exhaled as hard as he could, and wormed his way forwards from side to side, kicking with his toes and digging his fingernails into the rock. He felt a breeze on his face and sensed the cold smell of water. His fingertips felt the lip of the tunnel and he pulled himself free.

Gregor was in a black cavernous space where droplets echoed around him as they fell into water. The rocks were slippery, covered in slime. A broken thread of light swam towards him up a slow-moving stream. He went down on his hands and knees, sank his hands into the water and drank.

'You frightened them away,' said an accusing little voice. He made out the outline of a little girl sitting on a rock across the stream. 'This stream is called Stot,' she added. 'Do you like my cave?'

'Yes, it's fine,' said Gregor, drawing his sleeve across his mouth.

'Why did you come?' she asked. 'I was watching them playing with their golden balls. You drove them away. You're not one of them.'

'You're a silly girl,' said Gregor. 'Does your mother know you're here?'

'Taid knows,' she snapped back, jumping from her rock and skipping over the stream towards him. 'They won't come now, not while you're here. Let's go.' She held out her hand.

'You're so slow,' she complained, letting go his hand and running before him. 'You'll never catch me!'

Gregor struggled after her among the shadows and reflections. The thread of light had grown stronger and now swam like a trout up the stream. He could hear her shouting with delight some way in front. He reached the mouth of the cave where green daylight poured past leaves and branches and sparkled in the stream. Gregor thrust his head and shoulders out through thick foliage into a verdant wood of beech and oak. A light drizzle had beaded the young bracken. 'Where the hell did she go?' he muttered, scratching his head. Just then a hail of twigs stung his cheek followed by mischievous laughter. She hooted with delight as she crashed through the undergrowth away from him. 'He's coming, Taid,' he heard her shout. When he caught up with her she was standing at the foot of a round hillock hand in hand with the Du Traheus.

'Welcome, Gregor,' he said. 'You took your time. Come, I've a nice bottle of cherry brandy I'd like you to try.'

'Can you help me, Du Traheus?' said Gregor.

'That's another matter,' said the Du Traheus.

From a cleft in the hillock the Du Traheus produced a bottle and some glasses. There was an overhang close by with dry leaves to sit on. 'Let's drink to the memory of the old order, shall we?' They clinked glasses. The little girl had wandered off among the bluebells.

'You don't keep much of a check on your grand-daughter,' observed Gregor. 'Did you know she was in the cave?'

'Hunydd won't get lost in her own homeland,' replied the Du Traheus.

Wood pigeons cooed to one another. Gregor watched petals of sunlight filter through the canopy. In the grass by his feet he saw insects struggling among twigs and leaves. 'I'm trying to find Iwerydd,' he said.

'She's waiting for you,' said the Du Traheus. He drained his glass and filled both glasses up again.

'I'd do anything to see her smile and touch her hand.'

'Listen, Gregor,' said the Du Traheus thoughtfully. 'You got me the adder's stone that set me free, so if I can do something for you I'll do it. Unfortunately, it's going to take a bit of your time.'

'I don't care about that,' said Gregor. 'Just help me get back to her.'


Gregor followed the Du Traheus to the top of the rise. The old man sat cross-legged. He raised his adder stone in his right hand to catch the slanting rays of sun in its blue glass eye. Closing his eyes, he grasped Gregor's right hand in his left. 'I can see her pathways,' said the Du Traheus. 'You will see them too. But it will be up to you to reach her. You've already come a long way. You should know that yesterday is already quite a long time ago. I hope you find her and take good care of her. Have you closed your eyes?'

Gregor saw nothing save the usual red dots before his eyes. He wanted to see so much that he did not initially notice the ground slipping from under him. The river was silent. No birds chirruped. He was far away. It was night. There were lights below him on a dark ocean. An orange dawn filled one half of the sky. He was crossing a city coastline. Lights flowed across a bridge into the grid pattern of its streets. Thousands of squares of light shone from tall towers. He was closing on one tower block, high up towards a darkened window. Behind it lay an empty room. Moonlight filled the floor and cut diagonal shadows across the walls. The inner window sill shone in the moonlight in contrast to the dark rings of soil that lay on it. Tower blocks rose outside the window. The telephone rang. Gregor found it on a pile of phone books on the floor. He bent to pick up the receiver. There was no one there. He noticed a number written on the receiver. The handwriting was familiar. Close to the the phone books lay his old address book with its pencil in its spine and ragged ribbon. He picked it up and jotted down the phone number on a blank page. The apartment walls seemed to be becoming unstable. The moon outside was melting into a cloud. He tore out the page and scrunched it in his fist, placing the book back where he had found it. Darkness was falling over him. It seemed to suck him down into itself, as if he were a stone thrown into a marsh.

He heard again the rain's pitter-patter on young leaves. The river's roar fell upon his ears. Green light filled his open eyes. There was no one holding his hand. The Du Traheus was gone. As he turned his hand over and opened his fingers, the torn paper opened like a flower in his palm.

Gregor followed the path back along the river. He passed Dail Coed's mill which had scaffolding all around it. He could see no one. Likewise there was no one on the bridge or at the river's deep dark pools. He could smell no peat-smoke on the air. When he reached the farm gate he stood and stared at the brightly coloured bilingual sign that pointed to the farmhouse saying 'WHITE LAND OF HILLS FOLK MUSEUM'. On the front door a sign said 'WELCOME' in several languages. The warden looked up when Gregor stepped into the kitchen. 'Good afternoon,' he said curtly. 'You have your ticket, of course?'

'Of course,' said Gregor. The furniture was still the same; the dishes on the dresser; everything was in its place like a corpse in a coffin. Even the wireless set on the dresser - his radio - was still there. He crossed over and picked it up.

'No touching the exhibits,' commanded the warden getting up from his stool. 'That's a rare example of...'

'It's mine,' said Gregor. 'I left it here.'

'You did, did you? And when might that have been?'

'A few weeks ago,' said Gregor.

The warden's eyes narrowed. 'I've been here for three years and that radio set has been here all the time. Now put it back before I call security.'

Gregor shoved it into his arms. 'Have it,' he said. 'Do you have a phone here?'

'A telephone?' The warden looked astonished. 'That would be absolutely inappropriate. This is an authentic...'

Gregor was on his way out of the door.


Parked cars were heavy on the square. The houses were re-roofed. Windows were cleaned and polished. He strode across the square to the two great casks which now stood in the middle. Fibreglass pipers sat on top of them, their clothes coloured a garish red and blue. He struck a knuckle against one of them. It made a hollow sound. Gregor had no desire to put any coins in the slot to hear them play. Two crows perched on the weather vein on the tower. Public bars and small souvenir shops surrounded the square. Some were called things like 'Thelittlevillageshoponthesquare" with all the words rolled into one. He aimed for the nearest bar. A swing sign advertized the Bydol Arms.

'Peint o chwerw,' said Gregor to the man behind the bar. 'Lle mae'r ffôn?'

The barman looked at him impassively. He leant forwards, resting his large hands either side of one of his pumps.

'Chwerw plîs,' said Gregor. 'A dwisio defnyddio'r ffôn.'

A fat youth at the pool table raised his head. 'Everyffingc okay, Dad?'

'Speak properly if you want to get served,' said the barman to Gregor.

'Peint,' said Gregor. He pointed to the bitter pump.

'No sweat, Garvin,' said the landlord to the fat boy. 'Bloke 'ere don't know how to speak proper, that's all.'

The son manoeuvred his belly off the table and walked over. 'Not looking for trouble, is he?' he asked in his high-pitched nasal voice. His knuckles were white around his cue. 'We don't get much trouble around here,' he said bringing his eyes up close to Gregor's face. 'But when we do it won't be nuffingc we can't 'andle.'

Gregor held his stare. The frustrations that had filled his life in recent times began to well up within him as he contemplated the fat youth. He was thinking about Iwerydd waiting for him. He was thinking about Alice and all the things he should have done. He was thinking about Petrog Spalpin. And he thought about Dail Coed and the life that had been lived here between these white hills. And in the fat boy's face he saw the future.

An expectant smile quivered on the boy's lips. Gregor was surprised how calm he felt in the knowledge that he was going to have to hurt him. 'Fedri di handlo hyn 'ta?' he said. His forehead smashed into the fat boy's face like a ball hitting a coconut at the fair. The boy swayed silently for a second or two, moaned once and collapsed in a heap, blood pouring between his fingers from his broken nose.

Gregor spat on the floor and walked out.


No one came after him. There was a telephone sign in a shop window.

'Fedri di newid deg dolar?'

'Oh, yes, fluently,' said the shopkeeper. 'Un, dau, tri, mam yn dal squirrel. Rwyt ti'n hoffi coffi? Yes, indeed, not much call for it now though, see like.'

'Teleffôn?' said Gregor making the sign for a telephone with his thumb and little finger, shaking a ten-dollar bill under the man's nose.

'True van hin,' said the man, handing Gregor some change.

Gregor got the crumpled paper and picked up the receiver. Having dropped some coins into the slot he pushed the buttons carefully, listening for the squeak between each one.

12

Somewhere in New York City's ocean of twilight a phone rings in an empty room. Like a phone ringing next to you on a busy station; like a parked car's alarm obstinately ringing on the street. Yes, it rings like last night's dream that you can't quite hold on to or call back to mind. Grains of soil and earth in circles on the windowsill vibrate and tremble on the waves of sound. Then suddenly there is silence. The grains are still and the insects venture forth from their crevices. The silence is broken by the scratching of a key, the scraping of feet, a bustling and fussing at the door. And here are shadows that fall on the pools of light on the floor. 'I'm sorry, Mam,' says the girl as she lets go of her mother's hand and runs towards the silent telephone on its pile of books. 'I know where I left it! Here it is!' She picks up the address book and shows it triumphantly. 'I found it, Mam,' 'Thank you, Hunydd darling,' says Iwerydd. 'Please don't play with mummy's things if you're going to go and lose them. And look, you've torn a page from it as well!' 'I'm sorry,' says Hunydd looking from wall to wall and out through the wide window. 'This isn't our place any more, is it, Mam?' Before Iwerydd can answer, the phone rings again and she freezes. The phone is ringing, plundering the emptiness, breaking up the hour into thousands of points of time. When she sees her daughter reaching for it she finds her voice. 'Don't answer it, Hunydd.' Her voice is hard. This time should not exist. They are no longer here. The door is supposed to be closed behind them. But Hunydd likes to answer the phone. 'Hello!' she says, 'who is it?' She places her hand over the mouthpiece. 'He wants you, Mam.'

In downtown Manhattan, at the top of Fifth Avenue, you come to a wide leafy square with a white marble arch rising at its centre. Next to the arch you see a statue of the first president and on the far side stands Garibaldi on his pedestal. The students say that he turns his head whenever a virtuous girl walks past. This afternoon, like every afternoon, the square is full of people, locals and tourists, students and lovers, performers and acrobats, jugglers and clowns. A soapbox orator, passionate and loud; beyond him the fire-eaters and the fire-catchers in their costumes of silver, blue and gold. Roller-bladers skim, down-and-outs watch slowly, pigeons peck for crumbs between the paving stones. We don't see what causes them to rise up fluttering on the breeze to land clumsily on the marble arch. From here they can survey the world. From here the people seem to be following unseen paths that weave together and apart without ever touching hand or foot. Even as they brush past one another there is no more recognition between them than between the pigeons on the arch. Directly below we see a man with his back to the white marble, his head following the paths of the throng. He has not yet noticed a young mother and her daughter hand in hand on the edge of the square. The daughter is wearing red woollen mittens. Does he notice them now as they walk towards the arch? Finally he sees them, framed by strangers... he watches them as they cross towards him... they are hurrying towards him across the square. Now they have to stop to apologize for shoving someone... they try not to push and shove... but they knock into another person in their hurry to reach him. When they arrive, the little girl holds fast to her mother's hand. She turns to hide her face in the pleats of her mother's skirt. The mother bends to pick her up to her shoulder as the man takes a step towards them, his arms surrounding them in an embrace. The little girl still hides her face, only daring to peep out at him through the corner of her eye. He whispers something in her ear and she laughs and turns her bright smiling face towards him and lets him kiss her. The pigeons beat their wings noisily and fly from

their high fastness on the arch, a late sun burnish
wings, and land again on the square where they peck aw
more in search of crumbs.